SEVEN WONDERS JOURNALS

THE SELECT

✦

THE ORPHAN

BY PETER LERANGIS

First published in the USA by HarperCollins *Publishers Inc* 2014
First published in Great Britain by HarperCollins *Children's Books* 2014
HarperCollins *Children's Books* is a division of HarperCollins*Publishers* Ltd,
77-85 Fulham Palace Road, Hammersmith, London W6 8JB

Visit us on the web at
www.harpercollins.co.uk

1

Copyright © HarperCollins*Publishers* 2014

ISBN-13 978-0-00-758666-0

Printed and bound in England by
Clays Ltd, St Ives plc

Conditions of Sale

MIX
Paper from
responsible sources
FSC™ C007454

FSC™ is a non-profit international organisation established to promote
the responsible management of the world's forests. Products carrying the
FSC label are independently certified to assure consumers that they come
from forests that are managed to meet the social, economic and
ecological needs of present and future generations,
and other controlled sources.

Find out more about HarperCollins and the environment at
www.harpercollins.co.uk/green

The Seven Wonders series is a tale of adventure, sacrifice, and friendship. Of awesome mysteries locked away for centuries. Of prehistoric beasts and burping barefoot giants. Of an ordinary thirteen-year-old kid named Jack McKinley, captured and taken to a hidden place dedicated to the study of . . . him. You see, Jack is one of only four people who possess unearthly powers—powers that will kill them. To stay alive, these four friends must embark on a dangerous quest for the secrets of a lost civilization. The secrets they find may save them, but at a cost—the destruction of the world.

So what are these journals?

Well, first of all, the Seven Wonders series takes place now, with kids who might be your best friends. But recently, while working on the series, I came across a trove of documents that made my blood race. What do they have to do with this epic? An insane amount. After a high-level meeting in midtown Manhattan, and at some risk of personal danger, I have arranged for them to finally be released as soon as each is translated and ready.

The events in these journals occur centuries before the first book in the series, *The Colossus Rises*. The tales themselves are amazing. But more importantly, those who read them will have the inside track on everyone else. You'll learn some deep secrets—secrets some people might not want you to know.

A discovery like this is too big to hold back.

The fate of the world is in the balance.

 —PL

THE
SELECT

DAY BOOK AND JOURNAL

1894

BFW

THE JOURNAL OF

BURTON FRIEDRICH WENDERS

13 YRS OLD
SEPTEMBER 24, 1894

I DO NOT hear them, but I know they are near.

The creatures. The men. They hunt me through the rocks and jungle trees.

I must move, but I cannot. I fear my ankle is broken. If I stay, they will flush me out of this hiding place. When they are through with Father, they will come for me.

I pray they spare him. It is I whom they seek.

Yesterday I was the proud son of a renowned archaeologist, a man of science. We were explorers in a strange land. We would make incredible discoveries.

Today I know the truth.

Father brought me here to find a cure for my sickness. To heal my weakened body. To fix what science cannot understand.

But today I learned that my blood has sealed my fate.

5

If the prophecy is true, I will die before reaching my fourteenth birthday.

If the prophecy is true, I will cause the destruction of the world.

The island drew us here. It will draw others. Like Father. People who seek the truth. It must not end like this. So I leave this account for those who follow. And I pray, more than anything, that I have time to finish.

Our ship was called *Enigma*. She sailed ten days ago, September 14, into a red, swollen sun setting over Cardiff. But I lay in a cabin belowdecks, racked with head pain.

"Are you all right?" Father asked, peeking over for the dozenth time.

For the dozenth time I lied. "Yes."

"Then come abovedecks. The air will be good for you."

I followed him out of the cabin and up the ladder. Above and around us, the crew set the rigging, hauled in supplies, checked lists. English, French, Greek—their shouts kept my mind off the pain. Silently, I translated. What I didn't know, I learned from context. I had never heard the Malay tongue, but the words floated through the air in rapid cadences. They were spoken by a powerful but diminutive deckhand named Musa.

My love of languages is not why Father hired these

motley men. It was the only group he could get together in such a short time.

He knew the clock was ticking on my life.

Five weeks earlier I had collapsed during a cricket match. I thought I had been hit accidentally by a batsman. But when I awoke in a hospital, Father looked as if he had aged twenty years. He was talking to the doctor about a "mark."

I didn't know what he meant. But from that day, Father seemed transformed. The next two weeks he seemed like a madman—assembling a crew, scaring up funding for a sturdy ship. Impossible at such short notice! He was forced to interview vagabonds from shadows, to beg money from crooked lenders.

We sailed with a ragtag crew of paupers, criminals, and drunks. It was the best he could do.

As Father and I came abovedecks, I fought back nausea. The *Enigma* was a refitted whaling ship that stank of rancid blubber. Its planks creaked nastily on the water. Back at the port, Welsh dockmen mocked us in song: "Hail, *Enigma*, pump away! Drooping out of Cardiff Bay! Hear her as she cracks and groans! Next stop, mates, is Davy Jones!"

Our captain, a grizzled giant named Kurtz, hurled a lump of coal across the bay at them, nearly hitting one of the men. "Let me at them leek-lovin' cowards," he grumbled.

"Pay them no heed," Father said.

"Not that they're wrong, mind ye," Kurtz said, his eyes flashing with anger. "Us heading for the middle of the ocean to find nothing."

As he lumbered away, I looked at Father. My head pain was beginning to ease. "Why does he say this?" I asked.

Father took my arm and brought me to the wheelhouse. He took out an ancient map, marked with scribblings. In its center was a large *X*. Directly under that was an inscription in faded red letters, but as Father skillfully folded the map, the words were tucked away. "Kurtz sees no land under this mark, that's why," Father said. "But I know there is. The most important archaeological discovery I will ever make."

"Could not we have waited and gathered a better group of men?" I asked as I glanced toward the foremast, where two Portuguese sailors were brawling with Musa. As the Malay drew a dagger to protect himself, Father ran toward them.

He did not know that I had seen the inscription he'd folded away. It was in German: *Hier herrscht eine unvorstellbare Hölle.*

"Here lies a most unimaginable hell."

We reached our own *Hölle* early.

We were in open ocean. The sky was bright, the sails full, and the Strait of Gibraltar had long faded from sight. Eight days into the voyage, I was making progress in understanding Malay. Not to mention many of the saltier words and phrases used by these men in many other languages. I tried to help as often as I could, but the men treated me as if I were a small child. I must have seemed like one to them. My headaches were becoming more frequent, so I often went belowdecks to rest. Father would often join me for a card game or conversation.

It was during one of the games that we heard a scream above.

We raced upward. What we saw knocked us back on our heels.

The freshening sky had given way to an explosion of black clouds. They billowed toward us as if heaven itself had suddenly ruptured. Captain Kurtz was shoving sailors toward the mainsail sheets, shouting commands. First Mate Grendel, so quiet I'd thought he had no voice, was shrieking from the fo'c'sle, rousing the sailors.

The *Enigma* lurched upward. As it smacked back to the water, men fell to the deck. The wind sheared across the ship and the mainsail ripped down the center with a loud snap. In the thunder's boom, I stood, paralyzed, not knowing how to help. Rain pelted me from all directions. I saw a flash of lightning, followed by an unearthly crack. The mizzenmast split in two, falling toward me like a redwood. A hand gripped my forearm and I flew through the rain, tumbling to the deck with Father. As we rolled to safety, I saw the crumpled body of a sailor pinned to the deck by a jagged splinter of the mast.

I tried to help, but my feet slipped on the planks. The ship tilted to starboard as if launched by a catapult. I was airborne, flailing. All I saw beneath me was the sea, black and bubbling. Three sailors, screaming, disappeared into the water. I thought I would be propelled after them, but my shoulder caught the top of the gunwale railing. I cried out in pain, bouncing back hard to the deck.

"Sea monster!" a voice called out. "Sea monster!" It was the sailor named Llewellyn, dangling over the hull.

I held tight to the railing. Beneath me was a horrifying groan. I took it to be the strain on the keel's wood planking. I looked downward and saw the churn of a vast whirlpool.

In its center was a man's arm, quickly vanishing.

Where was Father? I looked around, suddenly terrified by the thought that the arm might have been his. But with relief I saw him coming toward me, clutching the railing. "Come!" he cried out.

He grabbed my forearm. The ship was rocking. I heard a deathly cry. Llewellyn's grip had loosened and he was dropping into the sea. I pulled away to try to grab him. "It's too late!" Father insisted, forcing me toward the battened-down hatch.

He yanked it open, shoving me toward the ladder. Overhead I thought I heard the flapping of wings. A frightening high-pitched chitter. "What is that?" I called out.

"Must be the angels, lost in the wind! Looking out for us!" Father shouted, trying desperately to be cheerful. "Now go!"

My fingers, wet and slippery, untwined from Father's. I fell from the ladder. Before my voice could form a cry, my head hit the deck below.

I awoke squinting.

To heat. To blaring light through the cabin porthole. The sun!

Immediately my heart jumped with relief. The storm, the whirlpool, the devilish noises—had it all been a dream?

I called for Father, but he was by my side. I felt his hand holding mine.

"How's the boy?" came First Mate Grendel's voice.

I willed my eyes fully open. Father's hair was a rat's nest, his face bruised, his spectacles gone. His shirt had torn and now hung in strips off his shoulders. I knew in that instant that the storm had been no dream.

Father chuckled and turned to Grendel, replying, "He's awake."

"Aye, good," Grendel said. "There'll be four of us, then."

I gripped Father's hand. The words chilled me. "Only four of us remain?" I asked.

"I thank God," Father said softly, "that I am holding the most important of them."

"We're not likely to last much longer if we can't rig the ship to sail again," Grendel said grimly. "And with the masts all snapped off, I don't—"

I heard a sudden shout from above. Musa. The fourth survivor.

"Can't understand the blasted fellow," Grendel said. "Too much trouble for him to learn English, I suppose—"

"'Land,'" I said.

Grendel stared at me. "Say what?"

"Musa," I explained. "He said, 'land.'"

Grendel raced away from us, up the ladder. Father followed, then I, on shaky legs.

Abovedecks, I nearly reeled backward from the intense daylight. Where roiling fists of blackness had smothered us, now the sun blazed in a dome of cotton-flecked blue. Musa's face was streaked with tears, his gap-toothed smile resembling the keys of a small piano. Dancing wildly, he gestured over the port bow.

On the watery horizon was a distant frosting of yellow green.

~~~~~~~~~~~~~~~

Schwenk. Coopersmith. Martins. Vizeu. Pappalas. Roark. Llewellyn. Finney. Gennaro. Caswell . . .

Grendel recited the sailors' names, placing for each a perfect seashell on a mound of sand. Reciting a prayer, he touched the white scrimshaw that hung around his neck on a leather strip: a crucifix carved into the cross section of a whale's tooth.

The battered *Enigma* lay anchored out to sea, tilted to starboard. It rocked on gentle swells, its timbers groaning in ghastly rhythm to Grendel's prayers. I felt the heat of the pink-yellow sand through the soles of my shoes. Behind us, a thick scrim of jungle greenery stretched in both directions. Animals cawed and screeched, unseen. A great mountain loomed in the distance, black and ominous, as if the storm itself had gathered to the spot and magically solidified.

Earlier we had managed to reach the shore via rowboat. All morning and into the afternoon we had traveled to and from our wounded ship, salvaging kerosene, sailcloth, wood, a small amount of salt beef and hardtack, a leather pack, a sopping wet blanket, and Father's revolver— the only firearm that had not been submerged in seawater and damaged. Miraculously I also found this journal, relatively dry and not yet used, which I put directly into my pocket—and a pencil. Everything else had either washed away or been ruined.

I had helped Musa and Grendel build four small tent huts, then briefly explored the jungle, finding a flat stone into which I scratched my name. Father had just unloaded and cleaned the gun, and he gave me a lesson in its use. He'd been unable to find extra ammunition, so we had only five bullets for hunting and protection. Accuracy would be essential. I was skittish about shooting, but Father scoffed. "Your aim was excellent when you were spitting wadded-up papers at your schoolmates!" he reminded me.

Now, as Grendel prayed, I bowed my head. But I could not concentrate due to a prickly sensation at the nape of my neck. I had the feeling I was being watched. I turned.

A shadow slipped from the trees toward Grendel.

"Behind you!" I cried out.

The little creature was swift, a scraggily monkey with one eye missing and a wicked grin. It snatched the scrimshaw from Grendel's neck, scooting back into the jungle with a triumphant, chattering cry.

Grendel bellowed a string of words I was not supposed to know. Grabbing the gun, he added, "I understand monkey meat's a grand delicacy, and I'm hungry. Who's coming with me?"

Father eyed him warily. "Can you shoot? We have too few bullets to waste on revenge."

"Marksman, highest level in the army," Grendel replied. "And I ain't planning to go far. Let me bring the boy. He'll learn something. And I'll return him safe and happy."

Father gave a firm no, but I reminded him I was no longer a child. That I would need to hunt, gather, and trap while we were here. I promised I would graduate from spitballs.

He softened at that, and instructed Grendel to exercise exceeding caution.

Off we went.

The jungle was oddly dark, its dense tree canopies blocking the afternoon sun. Grendel proved to be an expert tracker, using a pocketknife to carve blazes on trees. Before long we came to a glade, festooned with wildflowers. Just beyond it was a clear lagoon that bubbled fresh water. As I got closer, I saw fat golden fish swimming. They were meaty and beautiful. "We need a spear, not a gun," I said to Grendel, looking for a stick I could sharpen.

But Grendel's response was a forceful shove. I fell beside a thick tree. He ducked behind another. "Be invisible!" he warned.

Within moments, the bushes on the other side of the glade began to rustle. I saw a blur of brown gray and heard a snuffling, piglike sound. Then the lapping of water. I peeked around the tree. The animal's body was blocked by the brush, but its woolly haunches were enormous.

15

Grendel shot. I jumped away at the sound.

A bellowing cry rang out across the lagoon like nothing I'd ever heard—deep like an elephant's bleat, coarse like a lion's roar. "Blast it!" Grendel cried. "Shoddy firearms! He's getting away!"

I followed as he ran toward the lagoon. But the animal was gone. Not a sign.

Grendel stooped over a dark pool of blood and dipped his left hand into it. His fingers came up dripping.

Green.

"What the—?" With an abrupt cry, he plunged his hand into the lagoon. The water let out a sharp sizzle. His face twisted in pain, he pulled out his fingers and examined them in astonishment.

The skin was burned.

Balling his left hand into a fist, he secured the gun in his belt and pulled me away from the pool of green blood with his good hand.

What had we just seen? I shook as we walked deeper into the jungle. "It will be angry," I pointed out.

"That beast ain't natural," he said. "It could kill us all if we don't get it first."

Grendel stomped through the brush at a rapid clip, scowling. He had stopped marking blazes now. His injured hand was wrapped in his neckerchief, but I could tell from his grimace that it still hurt badly.

16

Through a break in the trees, I caught a glimpse of the black mountain. It was closer now, and taller than I'd thought.

Caws and screeches echoed in the thick foliage around us. Growing louder. The animals were warning one another, alarmed by the shot and the noise of our passage. I felt as if they were surrounding us, trying to scare us off.

But within that deafening din of alarm, I could hear another sound. Not an animal noise at all but a strange buzzing melody, made by instruments that sounded as if they used neither breath nor strings. It was barely audible, yet it cut through the wild animal cries as if plucking the very sinews of my body, vibrating the folds of my brain. "Do you hear that, Grendel?" I said. "The music?"

"Them beasts ain't music to me!" he said.

After another few minutes, though, Grendel's rage seemed to dim. The brush was too dense, and there was no sign of the injured beast. With a few choice curses, he announced we would return to camp. As we began to backtrack, Grendel held tightly to his burned hand. He wound through the jungle, pausing every few moments as if sniffing for a trail. His ways were a mystery to me, but within moments he was pointing to one of his earlier markings on a tree. "Blaze," he said.

We picked up speed. Glancing skyward, I noted with some alarm that the sun was low in the west. Night would be upon us soon, and I had no desire to be in this maze when darkness came.

We quickly passed the lagoon again, steering wide of the toxic blood. But at the edge, Grendel dropped unexpectedly to his knees.

On the other side of the clearing, the one-eyed monkey was jeering at us, swinging the scrimshaw like a chalice. "Me mum gave me that," Grendel growled.

He took aim and fired. I flinched. Grendel's aim looked to be true, but the monkey jerked aside as if it had predicted the bullet's path. It swung up into a tree and vanished into the darkness, jabbering.

Grendel ran after the creature. I scrambled to follow, but my foot caught on a root and I tumbled into a thicket of vines. I shouted Grendel's name.

For a moment I heard nothing. Then, from the direction where Grendel had gone, came a savage, saliva-choked animal roar.

Another shot rang out. Followed by Grendel's scream.

I ran to the sound. Vines tangled around me like witches' fingers but I ripped my way through.

I emerged into a small clearing. At the far edge lay the revolver on a bed of vines. A thick smear of green liquid led into the surrounding jungle.

Mixed with red.

I reached camp, hobbling and scratched by thorns. Over the water, the sun touched the horizon.

Musa had built a fire and was roasting a rather meager bird he'd snared. He hurried toward me, summoning Father from his tent. Their faces were taut with concern upon seeing me alone.

I showed him the gun, which I'd tucked into my belt. I described what had happened in the jungle.

Father took the gun and looked into the jungle. "Two bullets left," he said. "Let's find Grendel."

Musa began talking angrily, hands on hips. I translated for Father. "He says it will be dark in minutes. It would be suicide to go into the trees now."

Father looked at me oddly. His face seemed to be glowing. I could not quite read the expression. "How do you know this?" he asked. "You are good with languages, but in this short time, with no studies, no time for comparison and context . . . ?"

I shrugged, embarrassed to have my talents praised.

"I don't know. I suppose my skills have rather improved."

"Indeed they have." Father cupped his hand affectionately on my shoulder. Then, placing the gun securely in his belt, he gazed over the treetops to the black mountain. "We will set off tomorrow at sunrise."

We found a shoe. Just one.

In the clearing by the lagoon, the pool of blood had congealed and begun to flake. It was no longer green but black.

Musa had boldly led our morning trek, following Grendel's blazes. He was an expert at animal noises, shouting back to the birds and monkeys and keeping our spirits up. Now his face was drawn. He said he had never seen blood like this. He was worried that we had only two bullets.

I translated as he spoke, but Father's face was faraway, lost in thought. "We'll head for the mountain," he said.

Musa began to protest, but Father cut him off with a wave of the hand. "I know it's risky," he insisted, "but with Grendel gone we are in even greater danger. A signal sent from the top of the mountain will be seen much farther out to sea."

As I translated for Musa, Father began trekking into the jungle. Musa looked at me pleadingly. Skeptically. Continuing to the mountain meant miles through the treacherous jungle, followed by a climb that would take hours. At the top it appeared to be solid rock. We had no climbing equipment. The plan, to Musa, seemed insane.

I could not disagree. But Father was dead set, and so we trudged after him. Around us, the chattering grew louder. I began seeing jeering grins, wide eyes. A hard brown nut hurtled through the air. Ring-tailed monkeys, fossas, and lemurs—all began swinging from limbs, throwing nuts, rocks, feces. There were thirty or forty of them.

I felt something hit the back of my head and I jumped. I saw it fall to the ground: Grendel's scrimshaw necklace. Above us, the one-eyed monkey beat his chest, screaming.

"He is returning it," Musa said in Malay, his voice trembling. "He knows what happened to Grendel."

The leather strap was frayed and wet with monkey saliva. Nonetheless, I tied it around my neck, to honor our fallen comrade. I felt pity for his awful fate, but fear for our own. What manner of beast had killed him—and what if it came for us?

Ahead of us, Father seemed oblivious. He knelt by a rock formation, tearing vines from its surface. "Come!" he called. "Help me, Burt!"

My fingers shook as I helped him, but soon I became lost in the wonder of our discovery. It was a pile of ancient stone tablets—dozens!—etched with intricately carved images and symbols. Winged beasts with bodies like a lion. Giant warthoglike things. Flying monkeys. A complex round design that resembled a labyrinth. The etched symbols were tiny and impossibly neat, like hieroglyphics.

Father looked ecstatic. "This is it, Burt. All my life I've hoped these existed, and here they are! Look at these runes—influenced by ancient Egyptian . . . exhibiting elements of Asian pictographs and flourishes like a crude prototype of—"

"Altaic and Cyrillic script . . ." I said.

"We will camp here," he said, taking a pencil and pad from his pack.

"Here, Father?" I said, unable to control my astonishment.

"I must make copies before we continue," he replied. "Later you can help me decode these, Burt."

As I translated, Musa glowered in astonishment. "He expects us to go all the way up the mountain—and he wastes time with old rocks?"

I did not want to be caught in Musa's fury. I knew that trying to change Father's mind would be useless. But worse yet, my headache had begun to flare with renewed fury. It wasn't just caused by the monkey chatter and Musa's temper. No—like the distant hum of bees, the strange music had begun again. The music no one else seemed to hear: It pulsed with the jungle noises. Lights flashed behind my closed eyelids. I sat, hobbled by the pain.

Alarmed, Musa called for Father.

"Be right there," Father replied, hunched over the tablets.

"Father, I don't feel well . . ." It hurt to speak. My voice sounded high-pitched and feeble. Musa looked at me with concern.

Father mumbled something about taking a drink of water. I tried to answer him. I tried to get his attention away from his archaeology. But the music was growing louder, drowning out the monkeys, drowning out everything. Tendrils of sound pierced my brain like roots through soil.

I tried to stand up. I opened my mouth to cry out.

The last image I saw was the outstretched arms of Musa, trying to catch me as I passed out.

~~~~~~

I gasped and awoke from a horrific nightmare. In it, I was in a place much like this cursed island, chased by all manner of beasts—giant, slavering warthogs; flying raptors.

It was a relief to see Father's face.

Musa was building a fire at the edge of a clearing. He seemed withdrawn, angry. The sun had begun its descent into evening. The monkeys had quieted, but the music persisted in my head, as it had through my nightmare.

I struggled to sit up, my head still pounding. A thick blanket had been placed below me. I noticed that Father had piled the tablets around himself. His notebook was now filled with jottings, which he had clearly been working on while I was unconscious. He glanced at me distractedly and smiled, then looked back.

I was not expecting that. But something he'd said was stuck in my mind.

This is it, Burt. All my life I've hoped these existed.

It occurred to me, in a wave of revulsion, that this place had been our goal all along. We had reached the X on Father's map. And it was indeed a "most unimaginable hell."

Wenders the genius. Wenders the Great Discoverer. Wenders who stopped at nothing to get the great artifact.

"Is this why we are here?" I blurted out.

"Pardon?" Father said, momentarily distracted from his work.

"We rushed into a voyage without proper preparation, equipment, or personnel," I barreled on. "We sacrificed an entire ship's crew. Is this the price for your archaeology?"

Musa came closer, curious.

"There is a reason for this," Father said. "A good one. You will have to trust me, Burt."

"Trust you?" I said. "After you led us to a place your own map warned you away from? I sit here, ill with tropical fever. I don't want to die on this island! Why couldn't you have left me at home?"

Father turned away. When he faced me again, his eyes were rimmed with tears. "It's not tropical fever, Burt."

I braced my back against a tree. This was not the reaction I had expected. "Then tell me, what is it?"

"Something else," Father replied. "It matters not, Burt. I do not want to stir fear—"

"I am already afraid!" I protested. "You raised me to be honest, Father. Can I no longer expect the same from you?"

Father replied in a halting voice, barely audible. "You have a rare disease, described in ancient texts. Those who suffer it bear an unmistakable physical marking on the back of the head. No one has survived past a very young age."

"Is there no medicine?" I asked, my voice dry with shock.

"There is no cure for this, Burt," Father said. "Except that which is in the texts. And as you know, there is a fine line between history and myth. The texts speak of an ancient healing power on a sacred island. Several of them corroborate the same location. And that location matches the place on the map."

I shook my head, hoping that this was some bizarre dream. Hoping that I could shake away the monkeys and the deadly green-acid-blood creatures and the infernal music. . . . "A sacred island? Ancient healing power? This is not science," I said. "These are stories, Father. When I was a child you taught me the difference!"

"Power traveling through wires, glass bulbs that transmit light, conversations carried across continents—these were once stories, too," Father replied. "The first requirement for any scientist, Burt, is an open mind."

I wanted to protest. I wanted to translate for Musa. To have him share my outrage and confusion. But Father took me by the shoulders and gently laid me down on the blanket. "You must sleep to regain your strength. Musa and I will protect you through the night. I will explain more in the morning, and we will continue."

I knew I could not slumber. I had to know more. I had to translate for Musa, who was tending the fire and trying to look unconcerned with our conversation.

But then my head touched the blanket, and I was fast asleep.

~~~~~~~~~~~~

I woke several hours later, with a start.

Had I heard something?

I sat up. My head was no longer pounding. My body, drenched in sweat, felt cool. The illness had broken.

The jungle seemed eerily silent. Gone were the chatterings and hootings that had filled our day. Gone, too, was the buzzing, murmuring music. It was as if the night itself held its breath.

Musa's fire had burned to coals. I could see him in the dim glow, dozing, curled up on the ground. I glanced around and made out Father's silhouette at the opposite rim of the clearing. He was clutching his revolver, his back propped against a tree.

Snoring.

"Father!" I called out.

He muttered something, his head lolling to the other side. They were both exhausted.

For our own safety, I would have to take the night shift. As I rose, intending to take the gun from Father, I spotted a movement in the woods behind him. Not so much a solid thing as a shift of blackness.

I heard a stick snap to my right. A high-pitched "eeeee." Behind me, Musa let out a brief yell. I spun around.

He wasn't where he had been. In the dim light of the coals, I saw his legs sliding into the black jungle.

I called his name, running after him. But I stopped at the edge, where the darkness began. Entering it would be a colossal mistake. I needed the gun, now. I leaped toward Father. I saw him awake with a start.

My shirt suddenly went taut, pulled from above. My feet left the ground, and I rose swiftly into the trees as if on marionette strings. The silence erupted into a chorus of earsplitting screams. I felt sharp, furry fingers closing around my arms and legs. The monkeys! They were pulling me, turning me around. I fought to free myself, but their strength was astounding. More swung toward me from the surrounding trees as if summoned—dozens of them. Below me, Father shouted in horror.

In the red light of the waning fire, I could see them exchanging palm fronds, twigs, ropelike vines. They jabbered to one another, eyes flashing, as they braided, twisted, and tied knots with speed and dexterity. Before I could understand what they were doing, they let their creation drop from the branch.

Then they pushed me over.

27

I screamed as I landed in the taut mesh they'd just woven. It was a carrying net, which they passed from monkey to monkey like relay racers as they swung from the branches. In jerking fits I glided over the jungle, rising higher and higher into the blackness. Father's anguished shouts soon faded, and I could see the gibbous moon peeking through the tree canopy.

In the dim light, the black mountain loomed nearer. The little creatures were tossing me now. Cackling. Playing. I tried to tear my way through the net, but it had been twisted into an impossibly tight mesh. I swung like a pendulum, smacking into trunks and branches. The monkeys' cries seemed to grow more excited now, rising in pitch and intensity as if in argument.

Finally I saw one monkey leap from a tree and sink its teeth into the arm of another who was holding me. The whole troupe quickly joined in, screeching and beating at one another.

They were fighting for my possession.

I curled into a ball and prayed.

The chanting came as a relief.

I had been swung and dropped, slung over shoulders, tossed like a ball. I did not know where they'd carried me, as it occurred in nearly complete darkness. Through the mesh I had seen only fur and occasional eyes and teeth.

When the net was removed, I was sitting on a smooth rock surface at the edge of a large hole. The monkeys quickly dismantled their sack, then used the vines to tie my arms behind my back. The air was quite a bit cooler here, and I could hear languid drips fall into the blackness below. Rock walls rose all around me, their crags seeming to shift and dance with the reflected flicker of candlelight.

Across the hole was a doorway into another chamber, cut into the wall. People were chanting in there, their shadows moving in the light. I heard the strange music, too.

The voices were chanting in harmony to it.

"Hello?" I called out across the hole.

My voice boomed out, echoing off the walls. I looked up into a rock ceiling high above. I was in an enclosed place, some sort of cavern. I had been so smothered by the monkeys and the net that I had no idea how I'd gotten there.

In reply, a wizened man appeared in the cave opening. His cragged face seemed to have been hewn out of the rock itself, and his wispy white hair hung down to a silken robe. A gold-filigreed sash hung over the man's shoulder with an intricately embroidered sun symbol. Under any other circumstance, I would have complimented his wardrobe. But the one-eyed monkey sat on the sash, grinning at me sassily.

The man's eyes rolled back into his head as he doddered toward me, and he held high a chalice so heavy that I was afraid it would break his frail arms. Behind him followed six other men, also chanting. The second carried an elaborately carved black sword on an embroidered cushion. I expected an orchestra to follow them, but their little cave appeared to be empty. The music, as always, was coming from nowhere.

And everywhere.

The old men circled the hole. The third in line had a small basket, from which the monkey pulled little stone tokens and dropped them into the hole. Each token landed with a loud, watery plop. So—a well.

"Who are you?" I pleaded, but they ignored me.

I edged away. Despite the horrific trip there, I felt oddly strong. The music, louder than ever, no longer hurt my head. In fact, for the first time in days my head did not ache at all.

As I listened to the strange guttural chant, the words seemed to arrange themselves inside my brain. Like the ingredients to a complex recipe, they flew through filters of grammar, structure, context, relationships. I was certain this was no language I'd ever heard before, but to my utter astonishment, I was beginning to understand it. Some of the words were obviously names—Qalani, Karai, Massarym—but I picked out "long-awaited visitor" . . . "select" . . . "sacrifice" . . . and something that sounded like the Greek letter lambda.

As they drew closer, I yanked at the bonds around my wrists. Yes. I felt a certain give. Talented as the monkeys were, they were better at weaving nets than binding wrists.

The men did not seem to see me. "Hoo ha, la la la!" I sang out, fearing that the men might be in some kind of sightless trance. Then I attempted their own language: "Where am I?" The words were awkward and thick on my tongue. "Who are you? Why am I here?"

Several of the priests gasped. The leader stopped. Close up, his face was almost transparent, a skull with a paper draping. If I could guess his age, I would start with one hundred and work upward. His eyes lit on me, seeming to return from some distant galaxy. I felt a sharp chill.

His ancient, creaky voice seemed little more than air. But he spoke slowly enough for me to understand. "I am R'amphos, high priest of the Great Qalani. You look on us with fear. With revulsion. You see us as we are now— broken, waiting. But a great time ago our people were abundant, our land fruitful, our leaders fair. We lived in balance and harmony."

"Waiting?" I said. "For what?"

"For the glorious completion of our long-awaited task," he replied. "A task granted to us by Qalani, whom we praise for allowing us to live to this day."

"Praise Qalani!" the other men shouted.

"Eeee!" the one-eyed monkey concurred.

R'amphos handed the chalice to the third priest. The second priest lifted the carved sword off its cushion and bowed low, presenting the weapon to R'amphos. He grabbed the massive hilt. Its blade was thick obsidian, etched with runes.

I tugged harder at my bonds. My wrists ached. "What is that for?" I asked.

The old man's face seemed to sag further. "You are a child. We know you mean no evil. But you have come to us according to the prophecy. And we cannot allow you to fulfill it. Please understand. It is for the good of all."

I was certain then that I had wandered into a kind of nightmare bedlam, an island sanatorium of the insane. Surely I could escape.

The bonds seemed to be loosening a bit, but not quite enough to work my hands free. As I struggled, R'amphos edged closer. Time. I needed more of it. Perhaps I could try to reason with him. Convince him he'd made a mistake. Argue and delay him.

"What prophecy?" I asked. "Tell me all. You owe me that at least, before murdering me."

"Not murder. Sacrifice." The old man paused, his eyes growing more watery. He did not look homicidal or deranged but wearily determined. "It is foretold that Qalani's child will return, riding the storm. He will be dying. And die he must. Because if he tries to save himself, he will, in time, destroy the world."

For a moment I went numb with shock. Riding the storm . . . dying . . . It was as if he knew—knew of our shipwreck, my illness.

No. He couldn't have. These things were coincidences. Guesses. Quasi-religious idiocy. I refused to be killed by these lunatics before Father had a chance to find the cure for my disease. I had to think clearly.

"Listen to me," I begged. "You have the wrong person. My mother is named Greta, not Qalani. Greta Wenders. It doesn't even sound close. My father's name is Herman."

R'amphos reached out toward me. I flinched as his cold, skeletal fingers gripped the side of my head and turned it. "You carry the mark," he said.

I pulled away. I could feel one of the vines snap. My hands had a little more give. I could move my fingers, work my wrists. . . . "What mark?" I asked.

"I am sorry," R'amphos replied. "I bear you no ill will, my child. But you see, this is a happy day. We all die. We become dust; we are missed by friends and family and then forgotten. But your death will bring life. You will be prevented from doing to the world what was done to the land of Qalani."

"But—but I—"

The chanting started again in earnest. The monkey

bounced eagerly, clapping its hands. R'amphos lifted high the sword and stepped toward me. He was so close I could smell a faint, musty odor from his silken robes.

I took a deep breath, raised my head high, said a prayer, and spat.

I had not lost my boyhood talent. The saliva jettisoned like a slingshot, directly into the monkey's one good eye.

Wailing, the creature jumped toward me, teeth bared. The priest staggered, thrown off-balance.

I pulled against my bonds with all my strength. With a snap, they came loose. I swung my right hand around toward the monkey as it grabbed for my face. Its teeth clamped down hard on the tangle of vines I held. I completed the arc, sending the sadistic little creature into the well.

I brought my leg up. The old man was surprisingly quick, but my knee clipped the blade at the hilt, sending it into the air.

It smashed against the stone wall and fell to the platform. In a flash, three of the priests were upon me. As I fended off one with a blow to his bony jaw, the others grabbed me from behind. They were wrinkled and liver spotted, yet their agility and strength overwhelmed me. First one arm, then the other, was pinned behind my back.

"I am not what you think I am!" I cried out.

R'amphos had picked up the sword and was stepping

toward me. "We will not be turned back," he rasped. "You must comply. For your own safety and that of everything you see."

I yanked myself left and right. They had me immobilized. I watched in utter horror as R'amphos raised the blade and brought it down.

"No!" I screamed.

But as the word ripped from my throat, I was blinded by two quick flashes of orange and white.

The blade seemed to disintegrate into the air as an explosion blasted through the chamber. "LET HIM GO, YOU MONGRELS!"

Father's voice rang out, seeming to come from all directions. He was running in from a dark opening to my right, smoke trailing from the barrel of his gun. In his other hand he held a flaming torch aloft, and he thrust it toward one of the priests.

The man screamed as his robe burst into flames. He jumped into the well below, his shrieks joining with the monkey's. My captors let go, running away from the new intruder. The second bullet must have struck another priest, who lay bleeding on the ground.

R'amphos turned toward Father. "You must allow us to complete the sacrifice!" he cried in his language, his voice plain through the pandemonium.

Although Father did not understand a word, he was not

at a loss for a reply. "Go suck on a rock," he said, pulling me toward the opening.

We ran through a tunnel that sloped sharply upward. At the top of the slope, the pathway forked a couple of times, but Father seemed to know where he was going. I followed him until we emerged into fresh air.

He stopped, doubled over with exhaustion. "Must . . . catch my breath . . ."

"Thank you, Father." I was relieved to be standing still, as my head pounded horribly. Taking the torch from him, I beat it against the rock wall until the flames died. The sun was rising now, and we wouldn't need it. "How did you find me?"

"The monkeys . . ." he replied. "Loud beasts, you know . . . not much for secrecy when they've got what they want . . . so I followed their yammering through the woods. . . . I nearly lost them. But eventually I found my way here."

He glanced back toward the opening. It appeared to be in the side of a rock cliff, roughly triangular and about six feet high. Beside it stood a massive stone that matched its shape, like a door that had been pulled aside.

"Are you all right, Son?" Father continued. "Did they harm you in any way?"

I held the back of my head. That seemed to ease the pain a bit. "The priest . . . he said—"

"Said?" Father cut in. His eyes were wide. "You understood him?"

"It was as if I learned the entire language in moments, just from the few words they chanted," I told him.

"Remarkable," he whispered.

Now the music was intensifying, as if summoning me back . . . back into the opening. My head felt as if it might explode. "Father, what is happening to me? What is going on? Why did those men want to kill me?" The story poured out—the prediction of my arrival, the deadly procession, the sword, the nonsense about my mother being named Qalani.

Father listened in silence. I was expecting outrage, surprise, shock. But he merely nodded. With growing horror, I saw that he did not look terribly surprised.

"He said that I was going to destroy the world, Father!" I cried out, finishing the tale.

That seemed to shake him. "What? That's absurd, Burt. Pay no mind to that superstitious claptrap. How could a mere boy destroy the world?"

"But the other things, the other parts of the prophecy—you seem to know them!" I blurted out. "It seemed like you recognized the story!"

Father looked away.

"'He will be dying. And die he must'—that is what the priest said," I recounted. "Is it true, Father?"

He bowed his head. In a silence that lasted maybe three seconds, I felt an epoch go by. "There are . . . things I should tell you," he began.

The sound of distant shouting made him stop. I saw a flicker of light from inside the black triangle. Father's eyes widened with alarm. "Run!" he cried.

We took to the woods. The voices were close behind us now. The priests had found the entrance. Father and I charged through the brush, but the old men were surprisingly swift, and they knew the terrain. As we burst into a clearing, one of them emerged from behind a tree—ahead of us.

We stopped. Three other priests were at our backs. One of them carried a long wooden pole, while another was brandishing a fist-sized rock. The third was the fellow whose robe had caught fire. It hung from his shoulders, a blackened, sodden mess. The hair on one side of his head had also been singed away. "Release the boy," the priest said in the ancient language.

Father raised the gun.

"Stay back," I replied in the same tongue. "We have no wish to harm you. But if you try to take me, we will."

The priests hesitated. Then the burned one hurled himself at Father. With a curse, Father squeezed the trigger.

CLICK.

The gun was out of bullets.

The priest landed upon Father, yelling in fierce triumph.

38

As the two of them rolled on the ground, the other three advanced on me. I backed away.

"Go, Burt!" Father said.

"No!" I protested. "I won't leave you!"

"I'll be fine," he insisted. "It's you they want! Run! Lose them in the jungle! I'll find you at the shore camp."

My heart ached. Leaving him went against everything I felt and believed. But I knew he was right.

"Go!" Father repeated. "I will find you!"

I turned and ran. I was traveling blind, pointed in the vague direction of the shore. My foot clipped a root, and I fell with an involuntary shout.

Picking myself up, I raced on. My ankle twinged sharply; I had twisted it as I fell. Around me, the cawing of birds was like a mocking chorus. They seemed to be scolding me, giving voice to what my heart and soul were feeling.

I went as far as my ankle would allow, before it began to throb painfully. I ducked into the shelter of a bramble-choked rock outcropping.

This outcropping. Where I sit now. Where worms poke their heads lazily from the soil, and grubs burrow into the mossy tufts between rocks. They will be here tomorrow, too. And the next day and the next century.

I will not.

I have felt safe while writing this. But the sun will go down, and the priests will not rest until they find me. I

39

must return to the camp. I must find Father.

If he does not live, I will be alone. If he lives, how long will I? Where is a cure for my disease in this place of ancient priests and green-blooded beasts and net-weaving monkeys?

What is this place?

Who am I?

I pray that he will find me soon. That before I die we will have time to discover a way to save me. To save the world, if the prophecy is true. Perhaps the secret is in deciphering the tablets. If not—if we die here—I hope it will not be in vain.

The birds have silenced. Something must be nearby.

I will attempt to bury this now for safekeeping, for I think I hear—

⤐ THE ⤜
ORPHAN

CHAPTER ONE

*GO, DARIA. NOW.

My knees shook. I stood before the gate of the King's Garden, trying not to look at the magnificent people who strolled in and out. I did not want my eyes, my face, to give me away. I hoped my clean tunic would fool them. I hoped that on this afternoon they would not see me as a street urchin, a slave, a *wardum*, a creature of the dirt.

My plan was crazy. But my friend Frada lay dying, and I needed to save her. I had to do the unthinkable. And fast. Pressing down the wrinkles of my garment, I held my head high and stepped through the gate.

I was greeted by a blast of bad breath. "Step aside!"

---

*Translated from Ancient Aramaic

43

bellowed a royal guard, dragging a large sack. "King Nabu-na'id the Great approaches!"

The king? Now?

I leaped back into the street, as the guard repeated the command in several languages—Anatolian, Greek, Akkadian, Judean, Persian. People from so many different lands had come to Babylon years ago, before Sippar came. Before Babylon had been cut off from the rest of the world. Over time, listening carefully, I had come to understand nearly all their tongues. A useful skill for one who must survive in the streets.

Looking up the hill I saw the royal chariot drawing near, attended by four miserable-looking slaves. The crowd stepped back, bowing low.

"Here it is, my lord and master!" the brutish guard yelled. With a grunt, he threw the sack into the street, the Boulevard of the Gardens. "The last one!"

The bundle thumped heavily, raising a cloud of dust tinged with red.

Blood red.

The crowd surged forward to look. They pushed me aside, blocking my view. Gasps erupted all around. An old woman fell to her knees in shock. A small boy began to cry. I wriggled my way through, and soon I saw what the ragged sack really was—a man, dressed in tatters and beaten to a lump.

I turned away. In the reign of Nabu-na'id the Nasty,

violence was more plentiful than sunshine. As the chariot stopped, the king did not bother to glance downward. His beard, elaborately oiled and curled, glinted in the sun. "Bel-Shar-Usur," he barked, his voice like a dragon's rasp, "what says the rebel now?" Bel-Shar-Usur, the royal vizier, slid from his chariot seat. Although he was ancient and stooped, he was said to be the son of the king. His steely-gray eyes flitted wildly, as if each eyeball were possessed by an enraged, trapped insect—yet somehow, miraculously, he saw everything. Stepping toward the crumpled man, Bel-Shar-Usur used a gnarled olive-branch cane to turn him faceup. If the world were merciful, the man would be dead. But his eyes turned upward, showing unspeakable pain, as he muttered a tiny plea in the language of the Greeks. "Kind king, I am a father of four and have done nothing wrong."

"Wretched rebel," Bel-Shar-Usur said, "I'm afraid apologies are too late."

The king yawned and carefully, lavishly, picked his nose. By the look on his face, I could tell this action gave him great pleasure. "Dear Bel-Shar-Usur, you must properly learn the many languages of Babylon," he said, holding out his crusty finger for a slave to clean. "The rebel apologizes not. He speaks Persian. He tells me I stink like a dead lizard. Burn him—and let all Babylon know that the rebels have been eliminated!"

My heart sank as I tried to make sense of these lies. Both the king and his son had lied about the man's plea. He didn't apologize, he proclaimed his innocence—and he didn't speak Persian!

But what of the rebels—Zinn's warriors, the Children of Amytis—had they been eliminated? They were heroes to the common people, dreamers, masters of disguise and disruption. Their ancestors served the second Nabu-Kudurri-Usur, the Good King. Back then, they had been valued and encouraged. Now they were exiled and hunted by the royal guards. I had always dreamed of becoming one of them.

If they were truly dead, there was no hope.

As four slaves carried the victim away, the crowd gossiped. "What was his crime?" asked a woman with a kind, concerned face.

"The man is not a rebel," muttered a gray-bearded man with a Greek accent. He glanced toward the Royal Garden, its walls cascading with color, its flowers exploding with fresh scents. "Here was his crime: He clipped a small sprig of ivy to put in his little daughter's hair."

My knees turned to liquid. I had to grip a tree to keep from falling.

Beaten and condemned to death? For clipping a vine?

Over the walls, I could see a distant canopy of leaves. It was the Tree of Enchantment, whose magic pomegranates held awesome powers. Chewing their seeds could cure ills, give life to the sick. Guarded night and day from intruders, the tree was the king's most valued possession.

I was there that day on a mission. To save the life of my dying friend, Frada. To do what no one had ever done before.

I was going to steal one of the pomegranates.

CHAPTER TWO

THERE IS ONE cure for fear.

Insanity.

That was what I told myself as I stayed put, watching the chariot go away. I was crazy. I was temporarily not myself—no longer honest Daria, trustworthy Daria. Being a bit loose in the head, I could afford to be brave.

Did this make perfect sense? No. But the thought, strange though it was, gave me courage. I stepped boldly toward the gate.

And then I started shaking.

Thief! a voice cried in my head.

No. It was not thievery to save a friend's life. For weeks I'd tried to find a cure for Frada. I'd gathered remedies from

48

the markets, oily salves and herb tonics from apothecaries in exchange for running errands. Nothing had worked. If anything, she'd been getting worse. In the time of the Good King, all Babylonians partook of the fruit's magic. It was not thievery then. It was welcomed.

In a just world, it would still be thus. But we were in the time of Nabu-na'id now.

They beat to death a man who stole a tiny clipping! What will they do to someone who steals a magic pomegranate?

They would kill me. Of course. But did I have a choice? How could I live with myself if I allowed my friend to die?

I adjusted the empty pouch that hung from my belt. Carefully I drew a gray shawl around my head and tied it in place, to hide my blue eyes, bright red hair, and fair skin. Those qualities made me stand out in Babylon. On a day when I was about to break one of the king's most sacred laws, my appearance was like a bull's-eye on my back. Dressed as I was, I would look like any other girl—or even boy.

Go. Now. Before you lose your nerve.

I stepped through the gate.

The warmth and beauty filled me with hope. Pathways wound through arbors and among flower beds. Waves of fragrance, strong and exotic, wafted over me. And these were merely the formal outlying gardens, acres and acres surrounding the grandest achievement of Babylon—Mother's Mountain.

This was a structure of extraordinary height, spilling with the rarest and most colorful flowers. It was named for Queen Amytis, the wife of Nabu-Kudurri-Usur, who was called the Mother of All Babylonians. Nabu-na'id insisted we call it the Hanging Gardens, to erase the memory of the Good Queen. Now it loomed proudly in the distance. In a place so peaceful and lovely, how could there not be magic?

I stood close to a wealthy noble family, hoping people would think I was their servant. As soon as we were past the first bend, I peeled away. I wound through stone-paved paths, intoxicated by waves of perfume. When I reached a stone fountain, burbling with water spouted by stone fish, I stopped in my tracks.

There, rising high over my head, was the wall of the Inner Grove.

It was made of clay bricks and mortar, the height of at least three Darias. Guards marched to and fro, clad in gleaming metal chest pieces and headgear ornately crafted in bronze and iron. Each had a spear in hand and a sword on his belt. Any of these weapons could slice me quicker than I could open a pomegranate.

I stilled my pounding heart. But a person did not survive in the streets without wiles. I knew that my eyes were my best allies. I had to trust what I saw. I lingered by the fountain, pretending to daydream but watching fiercely.

The guards were bored and tired. They were also walking at a regular pace, back and forth, so that the closest section of the wall remained unguarded for . . . how long?

I counted slowly. At exactly the count of seven, a guard appeared again. Then he vanished and I counted again. Eight. That gave me a good idea of how much time I had.

Just above the wall I saw the spindly branches of a tree rising from the other side. If I climbed to the top, I could grab on and slide down inside. It would not hold the weight of a full-sized thief, but I am light—and fast.

I waited. The guards' footsteps receded, leaving the wall to me.

Go!

I leaped toward the wall, digging my work-toughened fingers and sandaled feet into the nooks, crannies, and vines. But they were tiny, and the wall was slickened by sap. I would never make it in time.

As I reached for the top, I heard rustling directly below me and felt my grip slipping.

The guard's voice shouted, *"What do you think you're doing?"* as I pulled myself up, ripping free the last vine I held.

CHAPTER THREE

MY EYES BLINKED open. I was on the ground. Facing upward.

I sprang to my feet. Where was he? Where was the guard?

I nearly jumped at the sound of his voice—but it was from the other side of the wall. I had fallen inside the Inner Grove. He could not see me, nor I him! "Hiding behind a bush—sleeping, Marcellus?" grunted the voice. I had to adjust it in my mind. He was speaking Judean. "I should report you!"

"But you won't," another voice replied, "because I'll tell the king you called him a fish-footed lizard!"

The two guards laughed. But in truth, they didn't care.

I suppose they disliked the king, too.

Most important, they hadn't seen me.

The air was damp and heavy. I glanced around. The king's Inner Grove was choked with plants, trees, shrubs, flowers, vines. I tried to feel good that I'd made it inside. There were places for me to hide, but my mind held only one thought:

What is hiding from me?

I saw shadows everywhere. I tried not to think about the Babylonian legends that passed in whispers at night. The Unspeakables. The monsters who were said to roam the grove at night, watching over Mother's Mountain—giant black birds with metal for skin, monkey-like creatures who spat fire—all were guarded by the biggest monster of all, the evil sightless Kranag.

Nonsense. Childish. Even when I was hardly old enough to carry a full water jug I didn't believe these tales.

I steeled myself, thought of Frada and how frail and near death she seemed, and I pushed forward, toward the Tree of Enchantment.

And then the dense brush ended abruptly, and there was the pomegranate tree. In the afternoon sun, its leaves seemed to dance with the passing breeze. I was no stranger to gardening. I had seen magnificent plants and trees before. I had coaxed dying plants into glorious life. But this was like a living, breathing being, as thick as clouds, as glorious as a song.

I drew closer, eyeing a half-dozen fist-sized fruits, right at my eye level. A tree that size should have carried dozens, maybe hundreds of pomegranates, but its offerings were few. Special and rare.

My fingers shook in the dappled sunlight as I reached out and pulled.

With a soft snap, the reddish-brown fruit came loose. I had it. The pomegranate was mine.

But before I could move away, I heard a strange, strangled sound. A hollow *Zoo-kulululu! Cack! Cack! Cack!* like a fierce roar forcing itself through a tiny slit. Whatever had caused it was inside the tree—behind a drooping branch in front of my eyes. What on earth could it be?

Run! screamed a voice in my head.

I should have listened to my instinct. I don't know what made me reach out, pull the leaves aside. Curiosity, I guess. Or maybe insanity. But when I did, I was staring into a knothole.

And two inky black eyes were staring back.

I stumbled back, nearly dropping the pomegranate. With a flutter of wings, a black creature flew out of the tree toward me. It had the mask of a wolf and the body of a hawk. Its feathers were a black so pure that it shone almost blue in the light. As I dropped to the ground, its feathers grazed my cheek. And then, with another screech, it was gone.

My heart pounded. I had startled it. It meant no harm. But as it flew over the tree canopies, surely the guards would see it. Would they suspect an intruder?

I had to move. I placed the pomegranate in the pouch that hung from my waist and ran to the wall, crashing through the underbrush.

On this side, the wall was sheer, polished to a smooth white luster. I could no easier climb it than fly over it. I glanced around desperately for a tree close to the wall. Something from which I could launch myself. But I could no longer see the place where I'd come in, and there were no trees here. The king's architect had been crafty, making it difficult to escape.

I ran blindly along the wall, hoping for a rough patch. A place where earthquakes had caused a section of the wall to crack, perhaps. But all I saw was smoothness, until I reached the entrance to the Inner Grove. The door was thick wood, reinforced by a metal gate. Framing it was a huge archway carved deeply with figures of beasts—lions, bulls, and the ancient mushushu that looked like both a lion and a lizard.

Footholds galore. It was practically a ladder for me. I couldn't help but grin as I grabbed onto the carvings and hoisted myself upward.

I paused at the top and looked down the other side. To

freedom. I was tempted to jump—but I knew if I did, I risked breaking an ankle. I looked around for something that would cushion my fall.

There. To my left, nearly thirty yards away, was a thin tree, fairly close to the wall. I could jump to it, and it would hold my weight. Then I'd climb safely down the other side.

As I shimmied across the top of the wall, I saw movement in the underbrush. I stiffened. A guard trundled out from under the tree. He was yawning, stretching, raising his face upward. In a moment he would see me. I flattened myself as much as I could. My heart beat so hard I feared it would shake the wall.

With an oddly high-pitched scream, the guard jumped backward. Had he seen me?

No. He was looking downward. I saw a flash of orange at his feet—a lizard skittering across his toes. Startled, the guard muttered angrily and hustled away on his rounds. I waited until he was out of sight, counted to three, and shimmied quickly along the top of the wall.

"Zoo-kulululu! Cack! Cack! Cack!" came a piercing shriek from above me.

The giant black wolf-bird landed on the wall, not ten feet away, blocking my path to the tree. It bent its neck toward me as if examining some strange specimen. "Shoo!" I whispered, but that just made it screech again.

I heard the thumping of footsteps. The guard was

approaching again. Instead, I aped the bird's song—"*Zoo-kulululu! Cack! Cack! Cack!*"—as loudly and shrilly as I could. It was startled for a moment, and I took the opportunity to push the bird aside and leap onto the nearby tree.

Half falling, half climbing, I made my way down the tree. I hit the ground in a roll and got immediately to my feet.

"You! Stop in the name of the king!"

The guard was tromping through the underbrush toward me, his spear twitching in his hand. Soon there would be others. Big, monstrous men with more strength than I would ever have.

But far, far less speed.

The pomegranate banged against my leg as I ran among the vines and trees. On the pathway I barged into the growing crowd of people who were leaving the garden to return home. The guard's shouts were growing distant now, causing a vague sense of confusion far behind me. My shawl fell to my neck as I bolted back through the outer gate.

And directly into the guard who had dragged the ragged man into the street.

"End of the run for you, street rat," he said, grabbing my arm.

CHAPTER FOUR

HOW HAD HE known?

I swallowed hard. The man towered over me. He was a beast. If I tried to run, he would yank my arm out of its socket. "I—I can explain!" I pleaded.

"Running through the garden is a safety hazard, little wretch," he said. "And it is against regulations."

"Running?" I squeaked.

And it dawned on me—he *didn't* know! How could he? He thought I was just a girl running recklessly for no reason. How could he know what I'd done? He had been on the outside.

I knew this was a stroke of dumb luck that would not last. I bowed low and spoke fast. "Yes, kind sir, you are right, and I will never do it again. . . ." But he was holding tight, not budging.

Frada's wise words came back to me: *To loosen a guard's will, feed his ego.*

". . . O pillar of great strength," I added. "And wisdom."

The corners of the guard's mouth turned upward into a proud, gap-toothed smile. His fingers went slack. And I stepped away—walking, not running, until I rounded the next bend, out of the guard's sight.

A voice boomed out from inside the garden. "What are you doing, fool? You call yourself a guardian of the gate? There is a pomegranate missing!" Running at full speed, I disappeared into the throng.

Soon I could hear at least three, maybe four guards behind me. But I had the advantage in the streets. They were my home. I sprinted down the road away from the gardens, through the ceremonial gate, and into the city. I raced past lavish houses I could never dream of entering. Many people were sympathetic to a vulnerable, running child, but others shouted my whereabouts to the guards. I darted into the vast outdoor market, hoping to lose them among the vendors. My eyes darted from stall to stall, looking for anything I could use to my advantage.

I tried to avoid looking at the gaunt, screaming man in the wooden stocks in the center of the market. His wrists and ankles were nearly worn through to the bone, bound by metal clamps. His face was bloodied and swollen. He had been there for five days, left to die because he had not bowed sufficiently to the king. My stomach wrenched at the sight, but there was nothing I could do. I had Frada to save.

I escaped out the opposite side of the market, into the streets. But the streets had guards, too. To "keep the peace," as the king labeled it. As they heard the shouts of my pursuers, they came after me, too. *"Capture the street rat! It stole the king's property!"*

My three pursuers became four, then eight. *It*, they called me. As if I were a thing, not a person. That notion just made me run faster.

I headed toward an alley, but one of them had gotten there first. I darted back into the street but I'd lost time. Now another set of guards was emerging from the road ahead. They were behind me and in front of me.

I stopped. There was only one way to go now.

Up.

Grabbing the window frame of the nearest shop, I hoisted myself onto a balcony. The wall was cracked and full of metal hooks left over from old signs. I used them as handholds to climb up the wall.

"Careful, Daria!" a voice shouted. "They are close behind!"

It was another urchin, a girl I knew only as Shirath,

who people called the sad-faced one. "Can you help me?" I shouted.

The girl didn't answer, but I knew the look in her eyes. In their expression I could read a kind of silent code shared only by street people: *I have your back.*

The guards followed, but they were slow and clumsy, weighted down by armor. I climbed to the roof and glanced in either direction. The shops were connected, so I could make it from building to building, easily jumping the difference in heights. This—this!—was the fastest way to move through the city. The breeze flowed freely through my thin tunic. With nothing but the distant towers and ziggurats in my line of sight, I felt swift and free.

"Halt or I will shoot!" a voice thundered behind me.

I turned. One of the guards had reached the roof and was aiming an arrow at my head. I knew in that moment that he really meant *Halt so I CAN shoot.*

So I shot first. With my sling.

I caught him square between the eyes. He let out a cry, arched backward, and fell. I cringed as I saw his body drop through the space between buildings—and land with a sickening splat into a pile of sheep manure.

He would live. But he wouldn't be bothering me.

With an effortful groan, another guard clambered onto the roof. I reached into my belt pouch to take out another stone.

I found nothing. I'd used the last one I had. Dropping the sling back into the pouch, I turned and ran across the roofs, leaping from building to building.

The guard was laughing. Taunting me. *"The lion gets the rat!"* he shouted.

I knew if he didn't catch me, he'd shoot me in the back. On an instinct, I darted left, across another row of rooftops with patched tiles and cracked surfaces—a poorer neighborhood.

A neighborhood I knew well. Very well.

As a small child, I'd lived in an old, abandoned place close to the city wall. I needed to get to it. Now. It was my only hope. It would save me.

I felt an arrow whoosh past my ear as I jumped from a higher building down onto the old shelter's roof. I landed near the wall shared by the two buildings. Carefully I walked sideways across the roof's edge. It was the last building on the block. If I jumped, I would be seriously hurt.

The guard appeared at the ledge above me. His chest heaved with the effort. When he saw I was trapped, he grinned.

"Nowhere to run now, thief," he said, leaping down toward the roof.

It was a strong leap. It launched him far forward. In midair, he drew his sword with a dramatic flourish. He landed with a loud thump, in the center of the roof.

I sidled farther along, my eyes on his feet. I knew that section of the roof well. It was rotted and patched with clay and netting. Unless, of course, it had been repaired.

"Please," I said. "You must hear me out! You're a father, are you not? Haven't you ever had a sick child?"

"You dare compare yourself to a child of a royal guard?" he replied, charging toward me. "Prepare to meet your maker, street raaaaaa—"

Just like that, he was gone.

Through the roof.

His shocked scream echoed upward as he fell down two stories of rotted wood onto the earthen floor below. Getting as close as I safely could, I peered through the hole into a silent, rising cloud of thick dust.

From far away came a muffled sound of commotion. I looked into the street. It was empty. The guards had taken another turn. In the confusion, they'd somehow been drawn off course. Unless . . .

Shirath. She must have done something to confuse them. Pointed the guards into another alley, perhaps, or sent them into a different quadrant. This was her way. I knew it in my soul. This was how we protected each other. In the absence of power, you had to use brains.

With no one chasing me now, I could lower myself over the edge of the wall, grabbing onto holes and window ledges. I landed quietly in a dark alley.

Alone at last. My chest burned. My body cramped. I stood with my back against the wall, trying to calm myself down. I'd eluded the guards for now, but I had to keep moving, just to be sure. Commotion had a way of shifting. Guards had a way of finding their prey.

As I rushed through the dark alley, I twisted my tunic until one arm and shoulder were bare and hung out through the same hole as my neck and head. It was a small adjustment, but it changed my silhouette. I spotted an old basket on the ground and picked it up as I passed by. Finally I wrapped the gray shawl back around my head, tucking my hair carefully inside.

By the time I walked into the sunlight, I looked nothing like the thief who had been fleeing over the rooftops.

I hummed as I made my way through the streets, trying to ignore the thumping of my heart.

The shops became more and more run-down as I walked, the lanes grimier. After a while, I was hit with the familiar smell of sewage. I breathed deeply and smiled. My worry fell away.

I was in the slums.

I took one last look over my shoulder before disappearing into an alleyway between two sturdy buildings. Near a dead-end, I turned into the area behind the buildings and came to the door I was looking for. I knocked softly.

A small voice came from inside, that of a boy pretending

to be much older than he actually was. "Go away. We are not accepting deliveries today."

Nico.

"It's me," I said.

When I heard a click from the other side, I pushed the door in. Startled, Nico stumbled backward. The sight of his gangly body, his shocked face with its shadow of a mustache someday to be, made me laugh aloud. Despite bright sunlight outside, the room was silent and dark, lit only by two small lamps, a place that held secrets. I closed and latched the door in a single motion, then collapsed against it, letting out a long breath.

Home at last.

CHAPTER FIVE

ZAKITI'S MIRACLE POTION Purveyors was a poor excuse for a wine shop, which sold a worse excuse for wine. The old lady who owned it had no access to vineyards, and thus no grapes. To earn our shelter, Nico, Frada, and I had to gather weeds and discarded fruit, which Zakiti somehow fermented into a potion so foul and stinking that it was a wonder anyone could stand it. But people did. At least enough to keep the small shop going.

We had no windows, only a few oil lamps to light the shop. Our beds were rarely twice in the same place. We moved them as needed, finding space among the barrels and equipment in the crowded room.

Nico leaned against a dusty brick wall to my left. His

eyes were deep and nearly black—always shifting, always calculating, always knowing something before you knew it. He wore a tunic made from a coarse brown sack that had once held lentils, and cinched with a rope. "Shirath told them you had sneaked to the northern quadrant," he said. "She saved your life."

"You knew?" I asked, astonished.

"Of course," he said. "And there had to be a reason the guards were after you, yes? So I also know what you must have in your pouch. Assuming this is true—because I have the best instincts in the city—I bow to you in awe."

Honestly, Nico could wear me out telling me how good, smart, and talented he is. "How is she?" I asked, moving toward a pallet of old sacks and blankets in one corner of the room.

Frada lay there limply. Her eyes were shut, her face skeletal, her mouse-brown hair a damp mess around her face

"Sleeping," Nico replied, "but hot to the touch."

I knelt closer to my good friend. Frada the Wise, Frada the Artist. She was unconscious but held a shard of charcoal in one hand. On the floor beside her was the side of a wooden crate, long ago broken off, which she liked to use as a drawing surface. On it was a half-finished drawing of three figures. Nico, Frada, Daria.

Frada liked to call us siblings. And who knew, maybe we were related. We knew nothing of where we came from. Ten years ago, someone had found us on the edge of Sippar, the black, roiling, moving wall of death that had come to surround the city. *Foundlings*, they called us. There was no place for us. Half the citizens of the city wouldn't even touch us, because we'd been so close to the deadly borders, as if that closeness were some kind of disease. And they were scared by the strange, white, angled mark on the back of my head.

So we got by on our own. And we would stick by one another always.

"Here, Frada," I said, eagerly pulling the pomegranate from my pouch. "Your troubles will be over."

Nico's eyes went wide at the sight of the fruit. "It's true! Frada, wake up! Look! The pomegranate!"

"Shsshhh, you want the entire neighborhood to know what I've got?" I said. "I've been chased by idiot guards through half the city. Find us a bowl and a knife so I can get this fruit open."

As Nico scurried off, Frada's head turned. She let out a stream of coughs. I held the pomegranate up to the light so she could see it. Her hazel eyes grew wide, glistening in the lamplight.

"*What's going on back here?*" shouted a voice like a scraping of a knife against stone. "I swear, if you've knocked over another cask I'll throw you into the street this time!"

Zakiti could have been anywhere from thirty to a

hundred. Her head was patched with matted clumps of brownish-gray hair, like a sun-scorched field. One of her eyes was dead, a milky sheen that stared into space. Years ago Zakiti had had a home, a good business, and fine looks. But on a visit to the Royal Garden she had been attacked by an escaped vizzeet, one of the monkey-like creatures whose foul spit can burn through skin. Banished into the street by a king who does not tolerate unsightliness, she came to be among those forced to keep their faces hidden in darkness.

Selling wine that was not really wine, Zakiti had grown used to a life of half-truths and outright lies. She could be kind or cruel. As long as we were quiet and did our work, we knew we had a roof over our heads.

I hid the pomegranate behind me. If Zakiti got mad, we'd be back on the streets.

"What do you have there, Daria?" The old lady hobbled into the storeroom, staring at us suspiciously with her one good eye. As she walked, tiny metal baubles jingled in her hair. Her clothes were threadbare and colorless.

I eyed Nico, who was skulking in the shadows, still looking for the bowl and knife. "Food," I said, head down. "For Frada."

Zakiti whipped her arm toward me, pulling at my elbow. "A pomegranate?" she whispered, her eye widening in astonishment. "Not from the King's Grove?"

"I—I can explain," I stammered.

She snatched the fruit away from me. As I looked on in horror, she pressed her fingers into the peel ever so slightly. "Why did you steal it?" Zakiti demanded. "Do you think this will bring you riches and status? Make you nobles? Take you away from me and make my life even more miserable?"

Frada let out a round of wracking coughs. A small trail of blood trickled down her cheek. She was dying before our eyes!

"It's not for us, Zakiti!" Nico said.

"*Lady* Zakiti!" the old crone spat.

"Lady Zakiti," I repeated. "Please. I took this for Frada. To bring her back to life. The pomegranate is said to cure ills."

"Oh . . . ?" Zakiti eyed me suspiciously.

"So you see—if she is well, you will again have three healthy workers," Nico added quickly, "not two!"

Zakiti scowled at Nico and me, then looked at Frada. "Do you think that is all I care about—workers? I can always get workers. Do you think me cold and inhuman? Pah!"

The old lady turned her back and walked away. Nico got ready to follow her, but I held him back.

She had left the pomegranate on a slanted, dusty table.

"You'll leave no trace of it here," she called out over her shoulder. "Not even its scent. If I find so much as a single seed, I'll turn you in to the king's guard. Oh, and when you're finished with Frada, go out and fetch me fruit from the market."

"Thank you"—Nico's voice was hushed with utter astonishment—"my lady."

"You will pay me back someday, I assure you," Zakiti said. "Now I must attend Serug the hunchback, who waits for his weekly purchase at the front door. I will endure his foul odor and rotten teeth today, out of respect for Frada. But this is the last time I do your work for you."

As she headed out of the room, I whispered to Nico, "She has a heart, after all."

"Encased deeply in rock," he replied. "But I am happy to see it."

Quickly he handed me the bowl. I placed the pomegranate inside and opened its skin with the knife. A sweet smell drifted up as I peeled back its rind, revealing plump, red seeds. Juice pilled out from the sides, making my mouth water. I was starving. But Frada came first. "Take these," I urged her. "Eat."

She turned, staring into the bowl with confusion. "Is it . . . really magic?" she said, her voice a raspy whisper.

"Yes," I said with a confidence I didn't have.

I forced one seed into her mouth. It was so full of juice it practically vibrated. As she bit down, juice trickled out between her teeth and down her cheeks.

Nico and I stared hopefully. I didn't know what to expect. Would she instantly get up and dance? Would it take days or weeks before the seeds took effect? Or would they ever? Perhaps their magic was a rumor, a figment of the king's twisted imagination.

Nothing changed in Frada's face. Her eyes remained unfocused, her voice slurred. ". . . ing," she said to me.

"What?" I replied.

She swallowed and tried again. "Sing, Daria."

I smiled. Frada loved my singing.

Nico, however, did not. He always made funny faces when I sang.

I ignored his taunting grin as I sang "Hope Is a Seed, Love Is a Garden." It is a tune about peace and prosperity, and it had become quite popular with the rebels. I brushed Frada's hair as I sang, keeping my voice low so Zakiti wouldn't hear.

Nico fed Frada pomegranate seeds slowly, one by one. "With a voice like yours, Daria," he said, "you should perform for the king."

I kicked him. "Do you ever stop insulting me?"

"That was meant to be a compliment!" he insisted. "You have no idea how difficult that was for me to do."

"I would sooner scream bloody murder in Nabu-na'id's ear," I said.

Soon Frada was full. She turned her head away and fell

back to sleep. Her breathing seemed less labored than it had been in the nights before. I touched her forehead. It was cooler. The fever was breaking.

"Nico . . ." I murmured. "It's . . . it's working!"

But Nico had drifted to sleep.

I thought about waking him to announce the good news, but I didn't have the heart. He looked so peaceful, and he had been working hard.

I felt shot through with energy. I figured I would run out to gather the fruit and weeds for Zakiti, while Nico stayed at Frada's side. I owed Zakiti. She had allowed us to save our friend's life.

Quietly, I gathered up the pomegranate skins. I would have to dispose of the evidence of my theft.

Night had fallen. The slums were lit by moonlight as I walked outside.

CHAPTER SIX

THE STINK GUIDED me.

I knew it well—rotten fruit, moldy leaves, half-digested vegetables. The ingredients that made Zakiti's Miracle Garden Wine. I followed my nose to a dark alleyway beside the ramshackle house of Taso the Great. He ran a food shop in the front of his house, where Babylonians rich and poor could find all manner of provisions. The "Great" part of his name referred to his generous belly, which had been known to get stuck in doorways.

At the end of the alleyway, I peeked around carefully, toward the rear of Taso's house. All the buildings here were perched at the top of a long, moat-like hole known as the Trough of Tears. In the times before Nabu-Kudurri-Usur, public enemies were tortured and thrown to their deaths here. Their cries were said to echo upward through the night, so that only the poor or hardhearted lived here now. I heard a door open and flattened myself to the wall.

Taso the Great emerged from his rear door, holding an enormous bucket nearly the size of his legendary belly. He lumbered to the edge of the cliff, and with a grunt tossed out the bucket's foul contents.

I waited until he was back inside, then tiptoed to the edge. What extraordinary luck—an old wooden ladder led downward into the pile of refuse. I could climb down and scoop the freshest layer off the top.

I lowered myself, guided by moonlight. I could see movement within the scraps, so I hissed, causing a team of rats to scurry away. They scolded me with angry squeaks as I climbed as far down as I could, holding my breath. I gripped the ladder tightly with one hand, and with the other I leaned down to scoop up a few handfuls of fruit peels and vegetable scraps. Stuffing them into my pouch, I scrambled back to the top.

A clopping of leather sandals rang out from the alleyway between buildings—a guard on patrol. Instead of returning on that path, I made my way across the ridge, skirting the backs of the houses. Most of them were empty and in disrepair, their occupants put to death by Nabu-na'id. It didn't take much to anger the king. Sometimes a poor appearance was enough to earn a guard's spear in your back.

With a voice like yours, Daria, you should be performing for the king. Nico's words infuriated me. The thought of entertaining the king made my stomach clench. It was a wonder that tyrant had not torched the slums. Given the choice of being kept by the king and living my wretched life, I'd take the wine shop and the streets. With Sippar surrounding us, the city was already prison enough. Who needed to live in a trap within a trap?

At the last house, I peered around carefully. I could hear the low murmur of conversation in the street. More guards? I couldn't be sure. I hid in the doorway of a mudbrick house.

A warm desert wind brought a fresh whiff of rot from below. In the distance I could see flickering light from some of the houses and from the palace ziggurat, spiraling upward. Past that, just beyond the bend of the horizon, was Sippar. The moving boundary that encircled Babylon. The black veil had descended many years ago. Sippar, which most thought of as certain death.

It was whispered around the city that I had actually come from Sippar, not just been found near it. I didn't believe that.

I didn't believe any of the myths about Sippar. A ring of death, past which nothing existed—it seemed the sort of thing you'd tell a child to keep her from playing in the woods. There was a world beyond the boundaries of the city, of that I was sure. Something more than this. A place that was truly our home.

The wind was unusually strong, and I feared a sandstorm. I curled my knees up to my chin as it became louder, until it sounded like the wailing of the dead.

CHAPTER SEVEN

I AWOKE TO a sky of dimming stars. Below me, the city winked up through the gathering light, as the night's blackness slowly gave way to a silvery predawn.

You fool! You weren't supposed to sleep!

I bolted to my feet. Stealing the pomegranate had been exhausting, but there was no excuse for my letting down my defenses. I could have been discovered by guards. Or by hungry beasts. Was Zakiti awake by now? She would be crazy with rage if she knew I was missing.

I raced along the backs of the buildings and onto the quiet streets. Through open windows I saw rumpled sacks inside the abandoned houses—the poor and neglected, Nabu-na'id's Nobodies. As I approached Zakiti's, I saw that the place was already lit by several lamps, which was odd for the early hour. I sneaked around back, assuming Zakiti was setting up for the day's work in the shop.

Frada was alone, lying on her pallet between two casks of wine. "Hello?" I said.

Her back was to me, and she turned slowly to reveal her face. Her eyes were shut, her features twisted, her hair matted by sweat. "Something . . ." she murmured ". . . approaches."

I crept closer. Nico was nowhere to be seen. "Not something—someone!" I said cheerily. "It's me! Daria. How are you feeling?"

". . . Not now, but in our lifetimes . . . we must not let it disturb our city . . ." Frada moaned. "The pomegranate brings . . . great change to us all."

I crouched beside her, brushing the salt-encrusted hair from her forehead. The fever had broken. Her eyes blinked. "Frada," I said gently, "it's all right. . . ."

As Frada stared at me, I could see fear draining from her eyes. "Daria . . . was it real? Was it real?"

I smiled. Her voice was stronger. I no longer heard a rattling in her lungs. "I don't know what you mean, dear Frada. You were dreaming. How do you feel?"

She sat up slowly, stretching her arms and legs, her joints popping. As her eyes darted around the room, I fought the urge to shriek with joy. Even these simple movements had been so far beyond her only hours earlier. "I feel . . . better."

A smile of disbelief spread across her face as she braced herself against the wall and slowly rose to her feet.

"Frada, look at you!" I said, wrapping her in a hug.

With a sharp bang, the alley door slammed open. I pulled away from Frada, nearly causing her to topple back onto the pallet. Zakiti hobbled in, sweating and breathing heavily. She had been out in the streets—during the day? It wasn't like her to leave the store after it had opened.

Her eyes bore into mine. "You did this to him!" she growled.

My heart dropped into my stomach. Nico. "Where is he?"

"Where were you?" Zakiti snapped. "Out getting ingredients—for the entire night? The boy was worried. He said he had fallen asleep, and when he woke you were gone. Impulsive fool!" As she paced the floor, I could hear her ancient joints cracking rhythmically. "He barely reached the end of the street when the king's guards took him. I followed. I told them I could not afford to lose a worker of his strength. I pleaded—"

"But why did they take him?" I asked. "He did nothing!"

She grabbed my hand, lifting my own fingers to my face. They were still stained bright red from the magic juice. "This is what they saw, you fool—evidence of the stolen pomegranate on his hands!"

I felt my knees buckle. They thought Nico had stolen the pomegranate!

He would be hauled to the dungeons. Common thieves had their hands cut off. But someone who had broken into the King's Grove and stolen from his prized possession— this was worse than treason. This was like slapping the king's face. Nico would be executed. Painfully. Publicly.

"This is my fault," I said. "I'll go to the captain of the guard and tell him that I was the one who stole the pomegranate. Nico is innocent."

"You are a worse fool than I thought!" Zakiti shot back. "They'll just arrest you, too—then both of you will be thrown before the king. I will be left with no able-bodied workers at all, just a dying . . ." Her eyes darted toward Frada for the first time, and the words choked in her mouth. "My dear girl . . . you look so much better!"

Frada nodded weakly, looking toward me for guidance. "We can't let them destroy Nico," she said.

"Of course not." I bolted toward the door. "I'm going to rescue him from the dungeons."

"How?" Frada asked.

"He's not in the dungeons, you muddleheaded girl!" Zakiti blurted out. "They would not be so merciful!"

I stopped in the doorway. The dungeons, merciful? What could be worse than the dungeons?

I thought of the beaten man at the edge of the Royal Gardens. The prisoner in the stocks. "The market . . ." I said, whirling toward Zakiti. "They brought him to the stocks, didn't they?"

She looked away, saying not a word.

As I fled the shop I could hear Frada's voice, still feeble: "Be careful, Daria . . ."

CHAPTER EIGHT

HE WASN'T IN the stocks.

He was lashed to a wooden stake. The sun bore down on his bruised, bloody face. Above him was a plank of wood with a single word written on it. I may have been a street rat, but I had taught myself to read, and I recognized the script: *Thief.*

No. Not Nico. I'm the thief. It should be me.

I stopped dead in my tracks. I felt as though the air had been sucked out of my lungs. I wanted to run toward him, to untie him and drag him back. But I knew we'd both be dead by the time my arm touched the rope.

Still, I had to do something. I *was* doing something. Moving into the square, as if my legs had a will of their

83

own. Every fiber of my being drew me closer to him—slowly, unobtrusively. My brain raced, trying to think of a plan. He would see me soon. Someone would notice.

A fist closed around my arm, yanking me backward. I lurched away, clenching my fists and ready to fight.

"Daria?" a lilting voice cried out.

I swallowed hard, looking into the deep brown eyes of my beloved singing instructor, Arwa. When I was a girl, she'd heard me singing in the streets and insisted on teaching me. For months, I had sneaked up to the conservatory's back entrance, where she would let me in secretly and teach me the technique of beautiful singing, how to support and relax, how to make words and melody fly like a spring breeze.

Now, in public, we had roles. She was a person of noble birth dressed in rich blue robes, an *awilum*. I was a street rat on the brink of despair. Our two classes of people did not interact in public. Ever. But she was pulling me along, touching the arm of an untouchable, in full sight of everyone. "T-that boy is Nico—" I stammered, digging in my heels, "my friend—"

With a strength I would not expect her to have, Arwa pulled me into a side street, where a handful of people went about their daily routines. "Follow me," she said. "It will appear as if you are my slave. And pretend we are having a routine conversation. You are a brilliant singer, Daria, and I will not let you sacrifice your life to your impulsiveness!

Of course I know who the boy is. The guards have count-less eyes on him right now. They're waiting to see if anyone tries to talk to him or help him. They know he did not take the pomegranate. They speak of someone with red hair. They suspect it may have been a small boy." She turned and raised a chiding eyebrow. "Or a girl."

We paused, shrouded in shadow, as I let her words sink in.

"Then I will sacrifice myself," I declared.

"And play right into their plan?" said Arwa with a scoff-ing laugh. "Over my corpse you will. That tyrant's wretched piece of fruit is not worth harming a hair on your head or the boy's. I will help you."

Arwa's eyes shone like torches in the shadow's dark-ness. I knew I should feel happy, grateful. But as good as I was at singing songs, I was never trained in the art of trusting people. Everyone in my life but Frada and Nico had failed me. "I am sorry, Arwa, but I do not need the help of others—"

She smiled. "You are as brave as you are talented. And as independent. But if you think I would betray my most beloved student to Nabu-na'id—that misshapen excuse for a human being—then you don't know me." Arwa dug a few coins from a pouch hanging from her belt and handed them to me, then gestured to my bare feet. "Buy sandals. The nicest ones you can afford."

"Sandals?" I said. "But why?"

"No questions now," Arwa said, looking nervously over her shoulder. "I will explain later. My students await. Meet me in the courtyard of the conservatory when my afternoon classes are over. If you have a clean appearance and are in good voice, my plan will work. We will free Nico."

"And—if it does not work?" I asked.

"The king will show you no mercy," Arwa said. "It is a good thing you are an orphan, Daria. Because if we fail, the king would track down your entire family and have them slaughtered. But I trust that fear for your own life is sufficient motivation. I will see you in a short while."

With that, she turned and walked away, leaving me slack-jawed in the dark alley.

CHAPTER NINE

TRACK DOWN YOUR entire family and have them slaughtered.

As I raced away, Arwa's statement seemed to echo like an evil taunt. What she did not realize was that I did have a family. To me, Nico and Frada were my brother and sister. No matter if I failed or succeeded in this mission, the king's men would know that I did it to save Nico. Would they then make the connection to Frada? Would they track her to Zakiti's shop? Someone would talk. Someone would give her away.

I knew I was supposed to go directly to the cobbler for sandals, but I had to see Frada. I had to warn her.

The sun was now climbing the eastern sky, but inside

Zakiti's shop it could have been the middle of the night. The lamplight gave Frada's sleeping figure a halo of gold. Her breaths were soft and even, free of the snores and moans that had attended her sickness. The pomegranate had been miraculous. Even in the short time I'd been away, she'd improved. Soon she would be back to her old self.

I could not let them hunt her down like an animal. She would have to go with me. If I could learn to trust Arwa, Frada must also trust me. Surely she could help in Arwa's mysterious plan.

Gently I touched the side of Frada's face. Her skin was warm. "Good morning," I said. "How are you feeling?"

"Daria?" Frada's eyes fluttered open. She sat up slowly, as if testing her own ability. "You're back! Did you find Nico?"

I quickly told her the story of his capture and of Arwa's offer to help. When I said I wanted to take her along, she did not hesitate to answer. "I will do it for you. For Nico. But, Daria, we must not forget about Zakiti. They will need to punish someone if we succeed. What if they come here and take their revenge on her?"

I admired Frada's deep empathy for others, but before I could think of a response, the old woman's voice cut through the murky darkness. "By the great Marduk, what is this I hear? Concern for old, broken-down Zakiti? You are leaving forever, to find that foolish boy, and you have a thought for me?"

Frada and I both froze. "I—I—" I stammered.

"Does the mushushu have your tongue?" Zakiti asked. "You have been nothing but trouble since the night I took you in. I should have thrown you out then."

"We are concerned, Lady Zakiti," Frada said, "that the king's guards will come after you."

Zakiti glared at her. "Concerned, are you? Tell me, who is our most regular customer? Give me his name!"

"Serug the Hunchback," I said, thinking of the ragged little drunken man who reported to our front door once a week.

Zakiti nodded. "Where do you suppose Serug gets his funds? The king's guards pay him to sneak my Miracle Garden Wine to the palace. Those brutes would no sooner give that up than bathe in vizzeet spit! Many are those who appreciate my secret recipes, dear child. No, I should have thrown you out because . . . because I knew this day would come. I knew this shop could not hold a girl like you."

"We will be leaving you without any workers," Frada remarked.

"Do you suppose you are so very important—that I would not have my pick of people desperate for work? Pah!" the old lady declared. But as she turned away, I thought I could see her eyes moisten. "Stay here. I'll pack provisions. And may Marduk be with you."

CHAPTER TEN

ARWA PULLED OPEN the conservatory's back door. Her eyes hardened at the sight of Frada. "Who is this?"

"This is Frada, my best friend," I said. "I trust her as if she were my sister. She has agreed—"

"Do you play or sing?" Arwa demanded. "Speak, girl. Your friend Daria has forced my hand and thus I must include you in this plan. Answer my question!"

I felt ashamed. Arwa had always been kind to me, but she believed in strict order and discipline, and she did not like surprises.

"I—I play the santur," Frada said tentatively.

"She taught herself," I added eagerly. "She accompanies me sometimes. Her hammer technique is perfect, attacking the strings so delicately—"

"That will have to do," Arwa said, cutting me off. She eyed our tunics, then stood back to look at our feet. I had managed to convince the cobbler to sell us two pairs of sandals for the money Arwa had given me. I worried that Arwa would laugh at my feet, which are wide and ill suited for shoes. Frada's slender feet, however, made her look like an *awilum.* "Very good," Arwa continued, "but your feet are filthy, both of you, and your tunics are threadbare. Go inside—now. I will find you more elegant clothing."

As she turned toward the conservatory building, Frada blurted out, "Arwa, please, what of Nico? Have you heard? Is he all right?"

Arwa spun around.

"Shush, girl. The walls have ears."

Aghast, Frada jumped away from the conservatory wall. "Ears? This is a place of great magic. . . ."

"It is an expression," I murmured.

Arwa produced a small wooden instrument from her pouch and held it before us. "Look as if I am teaching you something," she said softly as she fingered the holes with great exaggeration. "Your friend Nico is in a holding cell on the third level of the king's palace, the tower of Etemenanki. At the ground level are the king's chambers, and on the second are the guards' quarters. As you can see, this presents a problem of access."

"We would have been better off trying to free him in the center square!" I said.

"You would not be alive had you tried," Arwa said. "Listen carefully. Tonight the king is holding a magnificent feast. All the most important men and women of Babylon will be there. I've been commanded to provide music for part of the evening. You will sing, Daria. Frada and I will accompany you on santur and harp."

"Sing for the king?" I said with disgust. "I would rather kiss a lizard all night long."

"Then you and your lizard will be busy as the moon reaches its highest point," Arwa said calmly, "and you may not notice the criminals being marched into the center of the party. But I suspect you will recognize one of their screams as they are executed in front of the king's guests. Nico, you see, will be among them."

Frada gasped, staggering backward in shock. "The king would not do this—at a celebration!"

"It is his way of reminding the nobles what will happen if they ever dream of defying him," Arwa said flatly. "It is what we call terror, my dear. The province of the weak and cowardly."

No.

Nico, murdered in front of the wealthy *awilum*?

I felt faint. Frada's hand closed around my forearm. "I will sing," I said softly. "But the guards may recognize me as the one who stole the pomegranate."

"With a scarf on your head, those dolts will not know a thing," Arwa said. "With time, they will forget they ever saw you, even without a scarf. Their brains decay nightly with the effects of some poisonous wine delivered nightly by the hunchback Serug."

Frada and I shared a knowing glance. I could not stifle a laugh. "Zakiti's Miracle Garden Wine!" I exclaimed.

"Listen carefully," Arwa barreled onward. "You will meet a *wardum*, a slave woman named Nitacris. She oversees the female slaves at the palace. After you perform, pretend to be light-headed. Near fainting. The king will send you away with Nitacris. Her Aramaic is poor but she speaks fluently in the Anatolian tongue."

"I will understand either," I said.

"How can you be sure the king will act this way?" Frada asked.

"He's a music lover," Arwa replied. "He likes to seem generous to those he deems talented, and he will want you to recover quickly, to sing during the executions. But there will be no executions. Because Nitacris will take you to where Nico is. You will follow her instructions to the letter in order to rescue him. If you fail, we will not be playing music for Nico's execution tonight but waiting for our own. Am I understood?"

Frada nodded a little uncertainly. "Thank you, Arwa.

But . . . why are you doing this—risking your life for us? Asking nothing in return?"

Arwa's sharp glance caught us both up short. "My father was a noble who crossed the king. His crime? He was overheard speaking of Akitu, the annual celebration of the Babylonian god—"

"Marduk," Frada said. "Do you not think we are old enough to remember the festival? What great fun we had!"

"Until Nabu-na'id banned the celebration, and any mention of Marduk," Arwa said. "At a celebration like the one tonight, my father was beheaded—by surprise, as he was happily enjoying a roast. To set an example."

I did not know what to say. What a horrifying secret for Arwa to carry inside her!

"I believe in your talent, in your future—but no future is worth living under a murdering tyrant," Arwa went on, leaning forward. "So I am indeed asking for something: When you rescue Nico, consider joining us. The Children of Amytis."

"You are one of Zinn's rebels?" I asked. "But I heard they had all been—"

"Defeated?" Arwa laughed. "The king would have everyone believe so. But rumors do not become truths by magic. We are growing in number. Zinn and her lieutenants hide in the king's own hunting grounds—which he planted, tree by tree, irrigated by the Euphrates. They drink from his water and feast on his game. This rescue will be a slap in Nabu-na'id's face. He will know—the city will know—that the rebels are stronger than ever and the king's reign will soon be over."

I took a deep breath, letting the information sink in. Really, I just wanted to save Nico, not start a revolution.

"But what of us?" Frada asked. "Once the court has seen us, they'll not forget us."

"You will have some time before the court puts together what happened," Arwa replied. "In the meantime you will go straight to the hunting grounds, where the rebels will give you shelter and food. I've already sent word. When you arrive at the forest, remember this." Arwa whistled three precise birdsong notes. "That will let them know you're a friend."

"And if we decide not to join?" Frada asked.

Arwa shrugged wearily. "You can try to go back to your regular way of life. To Zakiti's. Perhaps adopt a disguise. Live the rest of your life as before. As a street rat picking through garbage with no hope of equality. The rebels will respect any decision you make. Now let us go. It's time you started bathing or we'll never get into the palace."

"Bathing?" I asked.

"When you are with Zinn, you may revel in the soil," Arwa said. "To be present at the king's court, you must wash."

CHAPTER ELEVEN

I HAD NOT expected that my "washing" would consist of a vigorous scraping of my skin, which was now an angry-looking pink. Arwa gave me a gauzy, pure-white tunic to wear, but even that fine material felt irritating.

"Lovely," Arwa said, tying a scarf the color of the bluest sky around my waist and a maroon veil around my head. "Look at yourself in the fountain, Daria."

At first I thought someone had cast a spell on the still water, replacing my reflected image with that of a princess. But it moved and grinned and laughed as I did.

"Is it you?" came a familiar voice, full of wonderment.

I turned to see a slender woman with Frada's eyes and smile, but her hair shone a lustrous golden brown, her skin smooth and pink hued. The signs of her illness—the mottled skin and matted hair, the emaciated frame—were gone as if she had never been sick in her life. "Frada, you are beautiful!"

"I wish we could admire ourselves all day, but we must move now," Arwa said. Quickly she reviewed our plan. Handing Frada a santur with two soft-malleted hammers, she led us out of the building.

The conservatory was in a cluster of structures on the opposite side of the Euphrates from the main part of the city. To reach Etemenanki, we crossed a bridge that gave us a spectacular view of Mother's Mountain. Although the magnificent hanging gardens were sealed off to the public by King Nabu-na'id, the aromas washed over us in cool, intoxicating gusts.

Passing through the grand tunnel of the Ishtar Gate, *wardum* and *awilum* alike bowed their heads to us. A skinny boy, Ashur, who always taunted me with jeers and disgusting noises, bowed to me without recognizing who I was.

The palace grounds were a maze of lush flowers, winding pathways, verdant bushes. Birds sang sweetly overhead, and pigs and goats scampered in pens along the perimeter. Bowing as they passed us, royal *wardum* scurried about carrying urns of oil and water, tending the grounds. Despite their hollow faces and bony limbs, they looked stronger than the street people we knew. A slave was worth nothing to the king unless "it" was in good health.

Up close, the tower of Etemenanki took my breath away. It soared to the sky, its tiers tapering to a point in the clouds. Such was the power of the structure I feared it would lift me upward, hurling me toward the heavens. Staircases led up along the outer walls that were covered in bright tiles, which depicted sacred Babylonian bulls and mushushus so realistic that I expected them to jump out. Every level of Etemenanki, right to the tapered top, was festooned with grand archways, statues, and carvings.

On one of those levels, I knew, was Nico.

"It must have taken years to build this," whispered Frada.

We passed through a guarded gate to a vast, enclosed courtyard, where men and women in fine, embroidered tunics stood laughing and drinking from jewel-encrusted glass goblets. They wore rings, bracelets, and necklaces of gold and silver, which glinted like bursts of flame, reflecting the setting sun.

They had put on their best to watch Nico be murdered. I hated them all.

Slaves stood in pairs along the walls. Most were girls. Their tunics were modest but clean and free of blemishes and holes. The male slaves wore turbans of bright colors. Most stood at attention, hands behind them. But some of the older ones were fussing over the placement of tables and chairs. The king had not yet arrived.

"There's Nitacris," Arwa whispered, nodding toward a woman near the archway that led into the palace. Nitacris was dressed in a maroon robe, her hair pulled back in a simple braid. She was quite beautiful, though years of slavery had cut deep lines in her face. She looked at Arwa and me for a fleeting moment before turning away. But I noticed a quick, subtle nod of the head, once . . . twice.

A slave appeared in the archway, blowing a brief triumphal fanfare on a hollow ram's horn. Falling instantly into a worshipful silence, the nobles turned and bowed.

It was strange how in a courtyard decorated with such treasures and art and finely dressed people, the king could be so repulsive. He entered aloft on a platform borne by four burly slaves, who carried him toward a golden throne cushioned by thick pillows. He yawned, his oiled beard momentarily resembling a crushed rat as it compressed downward into his neck. His turban shone with tiny jewels, and his long, brocade robe resembled a fine tapestry.

All this for a bony-faced man with bloodshot dark eyes and an expression of permanent disgust, as if he had mistakenly bitten into the remains of a dead bat.

To the king's right stood the captain of the guard, a tall, brawny giant with a thick lower lip, whom we only knew as Chtush, for the sound of his constant spitting. Around his waist he carried a massive pouch, made from the hide of a bull, which he set down heavily against a wall.

The sound made it clear that the pouch contained a bladed weapon, and that Chtush was the man who would carry out Nico's execution.

I could feel my cheeks flushing with rage. Arwa jabbed me gently in the ribs with her elbow. "Remember the plan," she whispered. "Do not let emotions blind you."

The king snapped his fingers and motioned to one of the female slaves. Hurrying over, she dropped to one knee. Then she pulled off one of his sandals, exposing a swollen foot that curved inward on itself like an injured animal. Without being told, she began to massage it. The king smiled.

I had to turn away. I don't know what was more revolting, the foot itself or the sight of the poor woman forced to touch it.

As Chtush approached, eyeing Frada and me warily, Arwa stepped forward.

"I know you are expecting only one performer," she said, "but these two are my most gifted students—particularly the singer."

Chtush spat and furrowed his brow as if assembling words in his mind very slowly, one by one. When he spoke, spittle flew from his mouth. His language was Akkadian, which was not the usual Aramaic language of the court. But I understood every word. "He says, 'Only one musician expected,'" I explained.

"Trust me, slave," Arwa said, "the king will be very impressed. And when he expresses this to me, I'll make sure he knows you're responsible."

As I translated, Chtush's face broke into a muscular smile that managed to release a thin line of saliva.

He pointed to an ornate harp set up next to Nabu-na'id's throne. Arwa sat and positioned her hands. Frada perched beside her on the ledge of a low brick wall and placed the santur on her lap.

Guests were lined up before the king, taking turns bowing to him and expressing their loyalty and good wishes. One by one, he dismissed them with a nod and a wave of a hand. I tried not to look at the poor *wardum* rubbing his swollen foot, but the putrid smell was a constant reminder.

As Arwa began playing softly, Nabu-na'id turned toward us. His eyes went from Arwa to Frada, where they rested for a moment. And then he looked at me, his lips curling upward in an expression that signaled delight but sickened me to my soul.

"This beauty is new," he said to Arwa, pointing a long, bony finger at me. "Show yourself to me, girl."

I stepped forward, holding my head high, trying not to betray what I was feeling inside.

"She will be a very special surprise, my king," Arwa said, speaking in a girlish, singsong fashion. "As beautiful as her face is, it cannot compare to her glorious voice."

101

The king smiled, then closed his eyes and grunted. I didn't know if that meant "go on" or perhaps it was a reaction to the foot massage.

Arwa began to strum again. Frada confidently struck the strings of the santur. The party slowly sank into a hush.

I took a deep breath, my eyes scanning the third level of the ziggurat, the tapered palace of Etemenanki. In the arched opening there I saw only shadows, but I knew Nico was there. He would hear me. He had to. And then he would recognize the voice. The voice he loved to mock and imitate. The voice that I would offer now to save his life.

Lift the back of your throat. Relax your neck and jaw. Support the breath with the strength of your abdomen. And most of all, mean the words that you sing with all your heart.

Arwa's instructions were etched into my brain. As I began, my voice echoed off the walls of Etemenanki, lifting into the night-bruised sky. I sang a tune that spoke of heroism and loyalty, death and enduring love. A murmur of approval spread through the crowd, and then a hush, until there wasn't a sound except the music. I could feel the king's eyes boring into the side of my head.

The last high note lingered long after I stopped, as if the sound itself had been trapped in the intricate carvings on the wall, destined to swirl and echo forever. As if the tower itself did not want to let the song go. After the last notes echoed away, a gust of applause rang out into the night.

"You have the voice of a goddess, child," the king said. Leaning forward, he jerked his bare foot, causing the slave girl to stumble backward. He beckoned me to approach. "Come, let me get a closer look at you."

Remember your mission, I commanded myself. Singing was easy, but faking an injury would be difficult. The king leered at me, and I fought back a wave of nausea.

Don't fight it—make use of that feeling.

I clutched my stomach. Below me was a crack in the floor and I purposefully jammed my toe into it. One of the slaves lurched forward instinctively and caught me by the elbow.

"What is this?" the king demanded.

"I feel faint," I said, fluttering my eyelashes.

Arwa rushed to my side. "Oh, dear," she said, "being in the presence of the king has taken her breath away."

"Ah yes, of course, this is to be expected," the king said. Snapping his fingers abruptly, he cried out, "Nitacris! Take this girl to a dressing chamber and let her rest. Give her whatever she needs. I want her to sing for us later. Something festive after the . . . ceremony."

Ceremony meant *executions*. I doubled over again.

A kind-looking older woman took my arm. As she led me away, I could hear Arwa playing the harp again. The king let out a loud belch, perfectly timed to a downbeat in the tune. "More wine!" he shouted. "Let us feast before the ceremony begins!"

Nitacris took me through the arched door and into the palace. It was a small antechamber that led to a hallway on one side and a long room on the other. "You are as good an actress," she whispered in a halting, thick accent, "as you are singing person."

"I can speak Anatolian," I said.

She smiled in surprise and launched into rapid speech in her own tongue:

"Listen to me carefully, then. Go to the end of the hallway, climb the back stairs to the second floor, and take a right. There, you'll see dressing chambers for the female slaves and beyond that, the baths. Use the stairs to the third floor. These stairs are open to all, but it's the only route I could arrange. If someone questions you, you got lost. If someone asks for me, feign ignorance."

"Where exactly will I find Nico?" I asked.

Nitacris pulled a small, triangular piece of metal from somewhere deep within her hair. It had been honed on one side to the sharpness of a sword blade. "Hide this in the folds of the scarf around your waist.

"Nico is being held with six rebel prisoners. They may not look it right now, but they're skilled rebel warriors— Children of Amytis. Slip this to one of them. Make sure no one sees you do it. Then keep the guards' attention. Once they've cut their bonds, the rebels will take over. You will escape directly down through the cooking area. Those who prepare the feast will be too busy to care about you. Most of them are loyal to the king, so beware."

"Keep the guards' attention?" I said. "How am I supposed to do this?"

"My child, you just left half the court breathless," Nitacris said. "Sing for them. Tell the guards you are sweetening the air, so that the condemned men will realize what beauty their treachery forces them to leave behind. Some nonsense like that. With a face and a voice like yours, they will believe anything."

As she turned to leave, I blurted out, "You aren't coming in with me?"

"If the rebellion is to succeed, we'll need someone inside the kingdom," she said. "I will tell the king you need a bit of time to recover. When the prisoners escape, he will suspect neither you nor me." She smiled and gave me a reassuring hug. "May Marduk look over you, my child. Whether you live or die. And I have confidence it will be the former."

As she scurried away, my own confidence crumbled into the dust.

CHAPTER TWELVE

"GO AWAY."

I stared into a pair of bloodshot brown eyes, peering through a slit in a thick wooden door. "I have been sent here by the king," I said as sweetly as I could, imitating the singsong voice that Arwa had used, "to enter this room and sing one last ballad to the prisoners before the . . . uh, ceremony."

"No one told me about this," the guard grunted.

"You can go ask the king yourself if you want," I said with a shrug. "I'll wait. But he wanted this to happen quickly, and you know how he is when underlings cause delays. Or I can simply report back that I was welcomed inside by the strong, handsome guard by the name of . . . ?"

I heard a click, and the door swung open. "Numa," he murmured.

Inside was a battered wooden table, where two other guards were tearing into the carcass of whatever animal had been their dinner. Each carried both a sword and a dagger on his belt. They barely looked up when I entered. "Thank you, kind Numa," I said. "Your obedience will be rewarded. . . ."

But the words were detached from meaning. Every one of my senses had gathered to focus on the long wooden bench against the far wall. There, half a dozen men in loincloths sat together, bruised, filthy, and dazed. From the red marks around their ankles, wrists, and necks, I assumed they'd been chained to dungeon walls for days. Their wrists were bound together in front of their stomachs with leather straps. None of them looked up to see me.

I had to examine their faces twice before I recognized Nico.

The breath caught in my throat. He was at the end of the row, his hair matted and stringy, his body hunched forward as he stared at the floor. He looked as if he had aged ten years.

"Get on with it," Numa said, his mouth full of meat.

"Yes, of course," I said. My voice faltered and I feared I would not be able to produce a sound.

Swallow. Breathe.

I began again. As the first notes left my mouth, Numa and his cohorts put down their meat. They stared at me, jaws agape, half-masticated food clumped on their thick tongues.

The prisoners stirred, and Nico looked up abruptly, as if waking from a dream. His eyes were those of a confused old man. Worried he would betray that he knew me, I cast him a warning glance and shook my head slightly.

He looked so weak and defeated. I wanted to wrap him in my arms, and I felt a hitch in my voice. *Do not let them see any emotion*, I commanded myself. *Get the weapon to the rebels—now!*

But how could I do that, in full view of the guards? Their eyes were fixed on me.

I could see the edge of my waist scarf swaying as I sang. I began to dance, letting my tunic billow outward. I turned my right side to the guards, moving my hips in rhythm, curling my hands and fingers in a complex pattern. Then I turned the other way.

As if it were part of the song, I began to whistle—the precise, three-note signal of the rebels.

Several of the prisoners sat up straighter. I could feel their eyes. Good. They knew.

Quickly, imperceptibly, I dipped my twirling fingers into the folds of the scarf I'd tied around my waist. I closed my thumb and first finger around the metal shard and cupped it in my palm. I could feel the blade cutting into my skin. It hurt. I would have to do this fast, before blood began to show.

"Do not approach these men!" Numa shouted, bolting up from the table. He placed himself between me and the prisoners.

This would not be as easy as I'd hoped. I began dancing more wildly, picking up the tempo of the song. I lifted up a metal plate and a ladle from the guards' table and beat them together. The guards began clapping and stomping their feet in rhythm, hooting with delight in spite of Numa's disapproval. He yelled at them to stop, waving his hands.

I tried to edge closer to the prisoners. But now the guards were leaping up from the table, dancing. Their beards glistening with animal fat, they jumped into the center of the room, blocking my way.

"Sit down, you fools!" Numa shouted.

"If the king and his fancy people can dance outside," one of the guards said, "so can we!"

"Especially if we have to clean up after the execution!" said another.

Through the clutch of thick bodies, I could see Nico's face. I could tell by the flash in his eyes that he knew what was happening—the execution, my plan, all of it. But my palm was dripping blood and he had noticed that, too. I dipped suddenly, sidling as close to him as I could, reaching out to give him the metal shard.

One of the clumsy guards thumped into me from the left side. The shard flew out of my hand in a spray of blood. The guard stopped for a moment and looked around as if a bug had just flown past. He was about to turn, when I hooked my arm through his and danced him in a circle. I raised my voice as loud as I could, nodding for him to join in. Where was Nico? I couldn't see him.

All the guards were singing now—all but Numa, who was yelling angrily at the top of his lungs. Had he seen? If he had the shard, we were all dead. He would use it to cut our throats one by one.

Out of the corner of my eye, I saw him approach, his face deep red. With a roar of anger, he threw aside the dancing guard.

"I know what you are doing," he said, "and it is time to silence the music."

He thrust out his arm and clutched my throat.

CHAPTER THIRTEEN

I COULD NO longer breathe. The guards had stopped dancing. One of them let out a shout.

As I dropped to my knees, I tried to pry Numa's hands from my throat, but they were like iron. My eyes rolled upward, and all I saw was black.

I felt a sudden blow from my left. I fell onto the floor, my throat free. I coughed violently, but I was being crushed by the body of a guard.

Scrambling desperately I slid out from underneath. I wheezed and gulped for breath, staggering under the table.

That was when I saw the filthy, bloodied feet—prisoners' bare feet, shuffling in the dirt along with the guards. I looked up into a chaos of fighting.

Three of the prisoners were free. Despite their ragged appearances and emaciated bodies, they were punching the guards, grabbing their weapons, biting, scratching, using every tactic at their disposal. Through the shifting bodies I could see the other prisoners, still on the bench. Nico was huddled with them, trying to work their bonds free with the metal shard.

I leaped across the room and took the shard from Nico. With free hands, I could slice into the bonds at a better angle. "I'm getting you out of here," I said.

"Daria . . ." he muttered, as much in disbelief as in gratitude. Up close, I could see how roughly he'd been treated. Bruises had formed around both eyes. His lip was fat and bloodied.

I worked my way through the thick rope until it snapped. The other two men, energized by the sudden freedom, plunged into the melee.

I took Nico's hand and made for the door. A prisoner fell in our path, crying out in pain. Numa stood over him, dagger poised. Nico grabbed his arm, but the guard just swatted him away. With a vengeful sneer, he came at me. "A rebel, are you?"

His neck bulged with anger—and I saw my opportunity. I pulled loose the scarf from my waist, swung it around his neck, and pulled as hard as I could.

Eyes bulging, he gagged and grabbed at the scarf. As he

sank to his knees, one of the prisoners brought a chair down over his head.

Numa fell in a heap, and I pulled back the scarf. The prisoner, looking at me in bafflement, said, "Who sent you?"

"Arwa," I replied. "And Nitacris. We must escape—"

"We will go through the kitchen and provide a distraction," he said, nodding quickly. "We'll charge through the front gate, into the party. Buy you some time while you escape."

"There are too many guards," I protested. "They'll slaughter you."

"I must stay and help my fellow prisoners," Nico began.

"If Nitacris said to go, you go," the prisoner replied. "Both of you. Now!"

Without missing a beat, he whirled around and clipped one of the guards on the jaw with a perfectly placed kick. The man fell to the floor, out cold.

"Nico, I think they can take care of themselves," I said.

As we ran into the hall, I could hear the pounding of footsteps coming up the stairs to our left—the stairs I had climbed minutes earlier. But Nitacris had told me to use the back stairs. I glanced around frantically. The hall was dark.

"It's there!" Nico said, pulling me toward a blind turn. "I know this hallway."

We ran around the corner and flew down a narrow,

dank set of stairs. Its walls were filthy, and a small rodent screamed at our surprise appearance, disappearing into a hole.

As we raced through the kitchen, Nico tore off a large, gleaming leg from a roast pig. "Thank you!" he cried out. Just as Nitacris had predicted, no one seemed to notice, so frantic were they about getting the food to the nobles.

It was not hard to find the back door, where the palace garbage was thrown daily into a ditch. The smell announced itself. As we ran for the door, Nico tore hungrily into the roast leg. "How can you eat *now*?" I shouted.

He grinned. "I think I'm the one who should be asking you questions," he said. "Like why are you dressed like that and how did you get in—"

Before he could finish the sentence, a broad figure stepped into the open doorway. We nearly fell in our attempt to stop.

Chtush stood staring at us, idling picking his teeth with the point of a dagger. "Roast boar," he said in Akkadian. "Very tasty."

As we staggered back, he wiped his dagger on his tunic. Then looking from Nico to me, he grinned. "What you did, songbird . . ." he said, his belly shaking with a deep chuckle. "Oh, what you did!"

Chtush put his dagger away safely. Could it be? Was Chtush on our side? A rebel?

I looked at Nico. He shrugged, tentatively joining in laughter, too. "Th-thank you," I said, inching toward the guard.

"One problem," Chtush said. "I was looking forward to the executions. To some good bloody fun."

He reached toward a kitchen table and lifted a bloodied cleaver. "So I will make my own fun. With you, right here. But first, little bird, sing your final song."

I opened my mouth. No sound came out.

"Sing!" Chtush bellowed. A string of saliva dropped from one side of his mouth as he stepped toward me.

"You're drooling," Nico said. "Hungry? Want some boar?"

As Chtush turned toward him, Nico threw the roast pig leg at his face. It splatted between his eyes and bounced away.

"Run, Daria!" Nico shouted.

I stood frozen to the spot as Chtush, with a cry of anger, raised the cleaver and lunged toward Nico.

CHAPTER FOURTEEN

THE CLEAVER FLASHED in the light. I thrust myself into its path. If Chtush was going to kill someone, let it be me. I heard a thud and felt myself falling.

I hit the ground, feeling crushed by an enormous weight. Chtush had fallen on top of me. He rolled away, screaming. I could smell something burning.

I saw Frada standing in the door, a broken oil lamp in her hands. "I—I just meant to knock him out, not to—"

Chtush leaped to his feet. His head was engulfed in flames. He slapped the fire with open palms, but it ignited the collar of his tunic, then quickly spread downward along his back. Chtush ran out into the night air, roaring with agony. We followed him. From the direction of the party, I could hear shouts and confusion. The king was screaming.

"Help me!" Chtush shouted, staggering toward the noise.

Two guards appeared, immediately tackling him. As they wrestled him to the ground, rolling him in the sandy soil, I grabbed Nico's and Frada's hands. "Come on!"

We ran to the palace wall. Nico, his body still racked from the beating, moved slower than usual. I boosted him and then Frada over the top.

As I hoisted myself over, my mind was reeling with what had just happened. Chtush would be fine—but he had seen us. As had all the prisoners' guards.

If they ever found any of us again, we were dead.

I landed next to Nico, who was grimacing with pain. "Can you run?" I asked him.

"Faster than both of you girls," he said.

Frada smiled. "Prove it."

We ran through the darkened streets, wanting to laugh at our newfound freedom but scared to draw attention. Some windows still shone with dull amber light, and I could hear the plaintive sounds of a flute here, a santur there. People making music with their families.

Real families.

I had always hoped to have one of my own. Now I knew that dream would never happen. I would have to settle for the rebels. And Nico and Frada.

All in all, I supposed things could be worse.

We paused at the edge of the king's hunting grounds. Here, the land changed dramatically. Babylon's arid, rocky soil gave way to a forest of tall trees. Nabu-na'id had spared no expense and sacrificed no fewer than nine *wardum*, who died in the backbreaking construction of this area. His plan was to stock it with animals for his hunting pleasure. But Zinn's rebels had adopted it as their home, hiding from sight and shooting the king's men at will with darts that rendered them unconscious. It was also rumored that the great mushushu, the animal that embodied the spirit of the god Marduk, was also loose in the woods.

Nowadays Nabu-na'id's men kept a safe distance.

As we entered the woods, I whistled the birdsong Arwa had taught me. "What are you doing?" Nico demanded. "You'll draw attention!"

"It is the rebel signal," I whispered. "When they hear it, they'll know we are friends." Nico fell to his knees and stood again. He was faltering. He'd been interrogated, tied up in the town square, beaten more than once, and assured that he was about to be killed all in one day. And now Frada and I had made him climb a wall and run a great distance from the city.

Frada, too, was breathing heavily. She'd only just

recovered from near death herself. The pomegranate had saved her life, but only time would bring her to full strength.

I pricked up my ears for the sound of approaching guards. Had they seen us? Would they suspect we'd be heading here?

I whistled again and again, desperate. In the darkness, the trees seemed like spindly hands enveloping us in a tight grip. Fragments of moonlight shone through the tree canopies, and I thought I could detect a movement to our left. "Follow me," I said.

But after a few steps I had to stop. From deeper in the forest came a strange noise. A hissing, as if a flock of birds had taken to the sky with snakes on their backs. In the noise's whoosh there were fleeting yawps and stuttering sounds like sped-up voices. "What's that?" Frada cried out.

"Isn't there s-s-somewhere else we could go?" Nico asked.

Out of the shadows leaped a figure from behind a rock. Despite the shadows, I could make out the sad, familiar face of a young girl. "The noise," she said, "is Sippar. It is drawing close tonight."

"Shirath!" I cried out.

She glanced from face to face. "We were not expecting three of you, Daria."

"But you—you're—" I stammered.

"A quiet street urchin?" she said with a smile. "Yes. And

an orphan, like you. And one of Zinn's warriors. All those things. You will be surprised at how many of us there are."

"You saved my life," I said.

"We work to save the good people of our great city," Shirath said. "Your friend appears to need care."

"Never felt better," Nico said with a groan.

Shirath nodded. "Come. Follow closely. We will heal you."

As she turned into the forest, Nico and Frada followed. I brought up the rear. But the hissing sound—the noise of Sippar—was seeping into my brain.

As wretched as it was, it seemed to be calling my name, beckoning to me.

Walk. Follow.

I shook the thought from my head and forced one foot in front of the other. Sippar was the Land of Death. Follow its call? What crazy notion was that? No one who had ever set foot in Sippar had survived.

Or had they?

Had anyone really tried to enter Sippar?

I thought about all the horrid stories about deaths caused by Sippar. In those stories, the victims were always traitors and rebels. People who would not obey the king.

Of course. Wouldn't this be another convenient lie for Nabu-na'id? Perhaps these people had not gone near Sippar at all. Perhaps they were executed, and their evil demise in Sippar was a lie, to keep Babylonians from trying to escape?

Ah, but no visitor from Persia, or anywhere else in the out-side world, has visited Babylon since Sippar appeared, a voice shouted inside my head.

But maybe Persians were cowering on the other side, just as afraid as we were. Afraid of the unknown. Maybe, on the other side, we would find shelter from Nabu-na'id.

Confronting the unknown took courage. And courage was the unwritten law of the streets.

I must at least see it.

I stopped. The hissing was like a physical thing inside my brain, pounding hard, obliterating all thought. I looked toward the sound. In the daylight I had seen Sippar, a dis-tant, waving curtain of black. Often it was too far away to see, but when it came close it had resembled a storm cloud containing black rain.

Now, in the forest's darkness, I could not see it at all. But I could feel it.

Shirath, Frada, and Nico had been swallowed up by the trees. In a moment they would notice I was missing. They would come back to find me. Shirath, no doubt, knew every inch of the hunting grounds.

I had to act fast.

As I stepped toward Sippar, I listened to its voices. I tried to make sense of the strange sounds and strange lan-guages. I heard blarings and clanking, high-pitched noises like strangled birds.

Images crowded into my brain, flashing with impossible speed—men and women in long black garments that wrapped around their legs, holding tiny boxes in their hands and thin strands coming from their ears. I saw carved metal sculptures that slid along hard black roads and stiff, shining birds in the sky. I saw ziggurats that made Etemenanki look tiny and farms the size of five Babylons. White boxes that opened outward with blasts of cool air, revealing food of impossible sweetness and coldness. People watching tiny versions of other people on flat surfaces, laughing, crying.

What were these things?

Go...

I could feel a wind kicking up around me. A penetrating heat. Sippar was burning me up and pulling me forward at the same time.

"Daria!"

Who? Who was that?

I tried to resist the pull. I tried to step back. I didn't know where Nico or Frada were. I didn't know where anything was. I only knew one thing. If I went any closer, I would be ripped apart.

I tried to reverse course, but my legs would not go back. I opened my mouth to protest, to scream. But I could not resist. Sippar was inevitable.

Sippar would be fed.

CHAPTER FIFTEEN

"GET BACK HERE, you idiot!" cried a guttural voice.

I felt something grip my shoulder. My body lurched backward. I landed in a tangle of limbs.

The strange dream images in my brain gave way to a rush of panic. I shook off the grip of enchantment.

"Get her far away!" another voice cried out.

I knew who that voice belonged to. A royal guard. They had found me, and one of them had me in his clutches. "Help!" I cried out, struggling to free myself.

"I am helping you!" the voice replied.

Numa. The prison guard.

He pulled me to my feet. I tried to spin around, to face him head-on, but he kept me turned away, both of us looking toward Sippar. The other guard was silhouetted in the moonlight. He was trying to run toward us but not moving. His eyes were wide with fear, his mouth open in a silent rictus.

His feet slowly left the ground. First his toes disappeared and then his calves. His body was being swallowed in blackness. As it engulfed his face, he let out a scream that seemed to stab me like a cold sword.

"No-o-o-o!" shouted Numa.

We staggered backward and fell. Numa struggled to his feet and grabbed me again. The noise was softening now. As quickly as it had rushed in, Sippar was receding.

"By the great Marduk . . ." Numa said, his voice parched and fearful. "We—we must go. Now."

In the dim light we could both see a black heap on the ground. I pulled out of Numa's grip. My body shook as if a giant hand had just twanged me like a harp string. "I—I don't think we're in danger now."

Both of us crept closer until we could make out the shape on the ground—a human figure, constructed completely of charred dust and fragments of bone and cloth.

CHAPTER SIXTEEN

NUMA'S FACE WAS hollow and scared, but he nevertheless pulled me roughly through the woods in the direction of the city. "The prisoner and the santur player—where are they?"

"Sippar," I lied. "Sippar swallowed them up, too."

Numa grunted. "It serves them right. It would have served you right, too. Now hurry. These woods are dangerous."

I nearly tripped over a root as we stumbled out of the forest and onto a road, where an ox-drawn cart was waiting. "Why didn't you let me go, then?" I asked.

Numa hoisted me into the cart. "You do not ask a royal guard questions, street rat!"

125

I kicked him in the knee and turned to run. But I felt something grab my ankle and I fell to the ground. My face scraped against the soil as my body was dragged back toward the cart. Numa had me at the end of a length of rope.

"Do not underestimate my skills," he said, quickly lifting me into the cart and tying me to the slatted walls with bonds of strong fabric. "I will tell you why I did not let you go—because I will delight in knowing that you face a worse fate than Sippar. The king wants to see you. Alive."

As the cart bounced back toward the palace in the darkness, I kicked and twisted, trying to free myself. But the knots were stronger than I was, and I finally gave in to exhaustion.

I had almost died. Numa, of all people, had saved me from oblivion. But now, as the spire of Etemenanki loomed closer, I wished he had let me go.

He was right. Death would be better than the king.

I spent the night on a cold dirt floor in the palace dungeon, awakened constantly by the chittering of rodents. I wondered if this was the room where they had kept Nico. The thought of him suffering here made me glad he had escaped into the care of the rebels. I could die here happy, knowing I'd saved him.

In my brief moments of sleep, I dreamed of Sippar. The

charred remains of the guard haunted me. I wondered if he had seen the same strange omens I had.

What was that place, anyway?

I knew one thing for sure—I would never, ever tempt that kind of closeness to Sippar again. And if I were to be separated from Nico and Frada for the rest of our lives, I prayed they would keep their distance, too.

But something had drawn me toward it. A vision of some strange world on the other side of the black death curtain. As if it had wanted me.

Was something really there? Was there another way to get through the blackness—a safer way?

Nonsense, I thought to myself as I finally fell asleep.

Early the next morning I was marched down the stairs by three royal guards. All of them had bruises and black eyes, and one of them walked with a pronounced limp. "Rough night?" I asked.

My only answer was a poke in the back, but I kept my balance.

I was shoved down a grand hallway with a stone floor and a magnificently tiled wall. The guards pushed me through an archway and threw me before the king, who sat on a luxurious throne atop a raised platform. A waif of a slave was on the ground before him, massaging his swollen, deformed foot.

Unlike my last presentation before the king, this time I had not been washed or prepared. My beautiful white tunic was torn and soiled with mud and grass. Bruises had already formed on my arms and legs, my braids were tangled, and I had lost my new sandals. Still, the king let out a high, tinny laugh when I appeared, like a child who'd just been offered a present.

He stroked his long beard, curling the end of it around one finger.

"Well, what does the street rat have to say for itself?" he asked.

I said nothing.

"You are guilty of high treason," the king said, licking his lips. "The death of many of my guards is on your pretty little head, not to mention the escape of several prisoners. And of course the loss into Sippar of your santur player and the street boy we captured in order to lure you to the palace—what was its name?"

"Nico was *his* name." I kept a stony face, but inside I felt victorious. The prisoners had escaped. Which meant that at least some of them were heading into the woods with the rebels. To join Nico and Frada.

My mission had succeeded.

"My king," I continued, "if I am to be put to death, let it be quick. I am ready."

The king threw his head back and laughed as if I had

tickled him with a giant feather. "Kill you and still the voice sweeter than all the flowers on Mother's Mountain? I think not. No, you have so much to offer me still."

He kicked away the slave girl and motioned to his disfigured foot.

"Take her place," he said to me. "Massage my foot."

I recoiled. "The thought of it makes me want to vomit. I would no sooner touch your wretched flesh than dine on pig manure. And the only singing you will hear from me will be this chant: *Down with the tyrant king!*"

Nabu-na'id sank back in his throne. "You know, I've been chatting with dear old Serug the Hunchback lately. He doesn't say much, but he knows quite a bit—for example, the location of the place where you have been living, dear Daria. That wine shop whose libations have been poisoning some of my own courtiers. A shop that is run by a decrepit old woman who, by rights, I could have beheaded."

"Zakiti has done nothing wrong!" I blurted out.

"Ah, I see. And would you say that about dear Arwa also? She comes from an *awilum* family and teaches the children of many other nobles. I don't imagine she was involved in your plot, was she?" The king sighed deeply, absently digging his finger into his nose, then wiping the results of his excavation onto the shoulder of a nearby slave.

"What are you going to do to them, you disgusting beast?" I demanded.

"Normally I'd have them executed just for being associated with you," the king replied, "but I believe they have their uses in this kingdom, and I am at heart a man of mercy. If you disobey me, if you fail to smile at me, if you call me by anything other than 'my king,' they are the ones who will suffer." He thrust his foot forward again. I could see his pea-sized, rotted toes wriggling through his sandal. "Come now, you have a job to do. You will make an excellent slave."

I sank to my knees and placed a hand on the king's foot. He let out a sigh.

Closing my eyes, I thought of Zakiti and Arwa. Of Nico, Frada, Shirath, and the freed prisoners. Of the rebels gathering in the forest. Of the world of Sippar, hovering mysteriously on the edges of Babylon. Of loyalty and mystery.

And family. Always family.

Nabu-na'id would not rule forever. Babylon would have another future. One in which the old values, the real values, were restored. I felt a smile warming my face.

"Ah, there we go . . ." the king murmured.

I was awash in happiness, and it mattered not what the king thought, or what I was doing. I began to sing. My voice took flight in the song that had helped Frada through her sickness, the song that people in the woods may have been singing at that moment, to give them strength.

"'Hope is a seed . . .'" I began.

The king sat up sharply. "What? Wait. That is the rebel song, is it not?"

"'Love is a garden . . .'" I continued, louder, my voice filling the chamber, my hands working the soothing salve into the skin of the king's foot.

"Stop that!" the king shouted. But his relief from pain was at war with his shock and anger, and he sank back into his throne with a satisfied snort. "Someone stop . . . that . . . girl . . ."

As my song soared, I could see the goggle-eyed Bel-Shar-Usur running in from an outer chamber. But the king's mouth was moving soundlessly, his eyes closed. No one interrupted the king when he was in this state. No one knew quite what to do.

So I kept singing. I sang as if my life depended on it.

It always had, and it always would.

READ A SNEAK PEEK OF BOOK THREE

CHAPTER ONE
THE VALLEY OF KINGS

FOR A DEAD PERSON, my mom looked amazing.

She had a few more gray hairs and wrinkles, which happens after six years, I guess. But her eyes and smile were exactly the same. Even in a cell phone image, those are the things you notice first.

"Jack?" said Aly Black, who was sitting next to me in the backseat of a rented car. "Are you okay?"

"Fine," I said. Which, honestly, was the biggest lie of my life. "I mean, for someone who's just discovered his mother faked her own death six years ago."

"Maybe she wasn't faking," said Cass Williams, sitting by the other door. "Maybe she survived. And had amnesia. Till now."

1

"Survived a fall into a crevasse in Antarctica?" I said.

I shut the phone. I had been looking at that photo nonstop since we escaped the Massa headquarters near the pyramids in Giza. I had shown it to everyone back in the Karai Institute, including Professor Bhegad, but I couldn't stay there. Not while she was here. Now we were returning to Egypt on a search to find her.

The car zipped down the Cairo–Alexandria highway in total silence. I wanted to be happy that Mom was alive. I wanted not to care that she had actually been off with a cult. But I wasn't and I did. Life had changed for me at age seven into a Before and After. Before was great. After was Dad on business trips all the time, me at home with one lame babysitter after the other, kids talking behind my back. I can count on one finger the number of times I went to a parent-teacher conference with an actual parent.

So you'll excuse me if I wasn't woo-hooing the fact that Mom had been hangin' out in a pyramid all this time with the Kings of Nasty. The people who stole our friend Marco and brainwashed him. The people who destroyed an entire civilization. The Slimeballs Whose Names Should Not Be Mentioned but I'll Do It Anyway. The Massa.

I turned back to the window, where the hot, gray-tan buildings of Giza raced by.

"Almost there," Torquin grunted. As he took the exit off the ring road, the right tires lifted off the ground and the

THE TOMB OF SHADOWS

left tires screeched. Aly and Cass slid into my side, and I
nearly dropped the phone. "Ohhhh . . ." groaned Cass.

"Um, Torquin?" Aly called out. "That left pedal? It's a
brake."

Torquin was nodding his head, pleased with the
maneuver. "Very smooth suspension. Very expensive car."

"Very nauseated passenger," Cass mumbled.

Torquin was the only person who could make a Lincoln
Town Car feel like a ride with the Flintstones. He is also
the only person I know who is over seven feet tall and who
never wears shoes.

"Are you okay, Cass?" Aly asked. "Are you going to
barf?"

"Don't say that," Cass said. "Just hearing the word barf
makes me want to barf."

"But you just said barf," Aly pointed out.

"*Gluurb*," went Cass.

I rolled down a window.

"I'm fine," Cass said, taking deep, gulping breaths.
"Just . . . f-f-fine."

Torquin slowed way down. I felt Aly's hand touching
mine. "You're nervous. Don't be. I'm glad we're doing this.
You were right to convince Professor Bhegad to let us, Jack."

Her voice was soft and gentle. She wore a gauzy, orangey
dress with a head covering, and contact lenses that turned
her blue eyes brown. I had to remind myself we were all

wearing disguises. Even me, with a dumb baseball cap that had a ponytail sewn into the back. After escaping the Massa a couple of days earlier and creating a big scene in town, we couldn't risk being recognized. "I am no longer Jack McKinley," I said. "My name is Faisal."

"Sorry." Aly smiled. "Anyway, we'll get through this. We've been through worse."

Worse? Maybe she meant being whisked away from our homes to an island institute in the middle of nowhere. Learning we'd inherited a gene from an Atlantean prince, which would give us superpowers before killing us by age fourteen. Being told that the only way to save our lives would be to find seven magic Atlantean orbs hidden in the Seven Wonders of the Ancient World—six of which don't exist anymore. It meant battling an ancient griffin, being betrayed by our friend Marco, watching a parallel world be destroyed.

I don't know if any of them qualified as worse than what we were about to do.

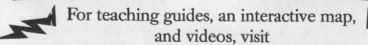